# Layers
# of
# Truth

**Steve McRoberts**

http://www.geocities.com/loyal2truth

Also by Steve McRoberts:

*Falling in Truth: The Education of a Jehovah's Witness*

*The Cure for Fundamentalism*

*Empathy Rising*

Available at www.lulu.com/smmcroberts

ISBN 978-1-4303-2633-5

www.geocities.com/loyal2truth

Published through Lulu, Inc.
3131 RDU Center, Suite 210
Morrisville, NC 27560
Printed in the U.S.A.

*For those who dare to peer beneath the surface.*

## Table of Contents

# Layer One

# 1
## *(Present day)*

"Can I ask you a question?" Mrs. Anderson said as she set the tea tray down in front of her guests: Dick and Pat Bradley.

She really hated asking this question; it might offend them, and she thought they made such a lovely couple, seated so prim and proper on her living-room sofa. They were always so well mannered, erudite, and nicely dressed. Pat's dress even matched the blues in the flowery design of the sofa's upholstery.

Dick exchanged a quick glance with Pat, which Mrs. Anderson could not read. Then he said, "Of course," as he took a cup and saucer and then balanced them precariously on his lap.

"We welcome questions," Pat added, beaming with delight.

Mrs. Anderson snuggled into a spot between the plethora of crocheted pillows on her overstuffed recliner. Then she looked at the floor, and sighed, as if reluctant to bring up a distasteful matter. At last she said: "Well, my pastor told me that you people once believed that King David had come back from the dead, and had even given a talk at one of your assemblies, but then one of your leaders murdered him, and served time in prison for it! Now, I know that can't be right—can it?"

"I'm glad you brought that up," Dick replied; "it gives us a chance to tell you the truth about what *really* happened."

"And the truth of the matter really proves that everything we've been teaching you is true," Pat said with an even broader smile.

"You see," Dick began, placing his teacup back on the tray so he could lean forward and tell his tale in earnest, "the *Watchman* had predicted way back in 1925 that King David and the other 'Ancient Worthies' such as Abraham, and Jacob, would be resurrected first, to help the brothers get through Armageddon."

"They even bought them a house!" Pat added, smiling harder than seemed humanly possible.

"Yes, and sure enough, in the year 2001, King David knocked on the door of that house!"

"A member of the Governing Body was there to greet him, too!" Pat said.

"Yes, and King David became one of us: a Jehovah's Watchman, and he spoke at several assemblies, announcing the start of the millennium—"

"Christ's thousand-year reign," Pat explained.

"Yes, I recall you telling me about that," Mrs. Anderson said in a doubtful tone.

"Well, everything was going well, and membership swelled," Dick continued. "The brothers and sisters were really excited to have finally witnessed the beginning of Armageddon and the millennium.

"But then a very unexpected thing happened: King David went apostate! He began questioning the authority of the Governing Body."

"So, Jehovah destroyed him," Pat said, "and disintegrated the body."

"Yes," Dick said, "and that was another validation of what we had always taught: that during the millennium apostates will be destroyed immediately by Jehovah without a trace remaining of their bodies."

"Because Jehovah doesn't want his people to have to be grave-diggers," Pat said.

"Of course the worldly people couldn't understand what was going on," Dick said, "all they could think of was that someone had murdered King David, and they needed a scapegoat to solve what they imagined was a crime.

"So they picked on a member of the Governing Body. Which was yet another proof that we're the right religion, because Jesus said we would be persecuted for his name."

"And it also fulfilled that Scripture in Revelation about one of Jehovah's Watchmen being in prison," Pat added.

"So, it's really very funny," Dick said with a forced laugh: "the clergy of Christendom try to use these facts *against* us when in reality they prove that we're the one true religion!"

"And any day now," Pat said with a confident smile, "more of the Ancient Worthies will appear at Beth-Sarim to help guide our work."

"Yes," Dick said, nodding his head exaggeratedly, as if he could make it all sound more likely by the sheer velocity of his nodding. "But the other Ancient Worthies that are resurrected will have to prove loyal to Jehovah and his organization, or they'll be destroyed as well."

"It just goes to show that no one is above the law of the Governing Body: God's organization here on Earth," Pat said.

# Layer Two

# 1
## *(September 2, 2001)*

The tinny voice on the cheap radio flooded the rental car's interior with the rapid-fire delivery of forced enthusiasm:

"Living up to its name, it's a beautiful sunny Sunday: fair skies, winds calm, and already a perfect sixty-nine degrees this morning. Coming up this hour, more top 100 hits on your Big Millennial Labor Day Weekend Countdown (try saying that five times real fast!)"

Bruce Kline shrugged and wondered why they bothered; it seemed it was always sixty-nine degrees here: a typical San Diego day. "Someday there will be perfect weather everywhere every day," he told the radio. He fell into such "witnessing" automatically now, after having done it steadily for most of his 69 years.

When the disc jockey began reading the day's horoscopes, Bruce shut the radio off in disgust.

"Can't get away from Satan even in your car," he muttered to himself.

He knocked his *2001 Yearbook* off the passenger seat as he fumbled for his *Kingdom Music* CD, and then had to give up when a blaring horn from the car next to him announced that Bruce had drifted across the line.

"Damn!" He shouted, quickly swerving fully back into his own lane.

He gave a sheepish look at the green minivan that now sped by him. Its driver, a young scowling woman, honked her horn with her right hand while aggressively thrusting her left middle finger in his direction.

He began to berate himself for having "sworn." But he soon consoled himself with the thought that at least he wasn't breaking the law by speeding (as the finger-toting woman decidedly was.) "If she hadn't been speeding," he said aloud to console himself, "then my 'accidental lane change' wouldn't have caused her a problem."

He sighed. In another minute he had cleared the incident from his mind.

He had more important things to think about. He had come all this way to make a presentation at the District Convention. The theme this year was "Keep Away From Unclean Thoughts." He was to give the keynote speech at one o'clock this afternoon to a packed Civic Center.

But he wasn't going directly there.

Craig Anderson, a lone brother living in Normal Heights, had put him up at his house during the convention. Several other families in the local congregations had vied for the privilege of housing a Governing Body member, but Bruce had chosen this lonely widower because he needed a break from the usual hubbub of a Watchman family. On this final day of the convention, he had gotten up early before Craig, wrote a quick thank-you note, grabbed his luggage, and headed out.

But instead of heading southwest towards the Convention Center, he was heading east along Adams Avenue—in order to indulge in a few moments of nostalgia.

His father had likewise been a member of the Governing Body. It was back when "Judge" Rutherford was president of the Society. His father had actually been with Rutherford when he died here in San Diego in 1942.

As he turned onto Braeburn Road, three men in a beat-up old car sped past in the opposite direction. "Bunch of worldly punks going way too fast," Bruce muttered, "No sense, and no hope."

Bruce pulled into the cul-de-sac that terminated Braeburn Road. He pulled to a stop directly in front of the house once known as Beth-Sarim: the House of Princes. The street address was neatly displayed on the short rock-and-mortar wall that lay to the right of the driveway: 4440.

It was a pity that the Society sold the house five years after Rutherford died. "Worldly people living there now," Bruce muttered as he frowned at the sight of the red sports car parked in the driveway plastered with bumper stickers promoting "Rock and Roll" radio stations.

Staring at the house and its yard, he began to reminisce. There was a sort of turret at the top of the house: a sunny round room where Rutherford had spent so much of his time writing his important final articles for the *Watchman*.

In the shuttered room, one floor down, Bruce had actually played a few times as a child, while his father visited the great man during his last days on earth.

In the front yard were the now tall palm trees he once had secretly shaken for a good ten minutes  (hoping for falling coconuts to no avail). In front of everything lay the massive cactus garden he had foolishly run into as a child: "My how I bled," he said aloud, and smiled at the memory of his father roughly bandaging and scolding him.

The reminiscing came to an abrupt halt. There, on the gradually sloping steps running between the rock wall and the driveway, a man was sitting.

Bruce hadn't noticed him at first because of the way the man blended in: white on white. The man was deathly pale, and dressed in a white toga. He wore a white headband decorated with a delicate, intricate pattern of gold.

The man appeared dazed. He sat staring for a long while. Eventually he shook his head and struggled to his feet. Bruce thought the man would walk towards him but instead he gathered up his toga, turned around, and headed up the stairs towards the house.

Bruce continued to watch, not knowing what to think as the man pounded on the door. "Could it be?" he wondered aloud.

No one answered the door after repeated attempts to rouse someone, and the man slowly, dejectedly, descended the stairs. When he got to the bottom he nearly collapsed, and sat down heavily on the bottom step.

Bruce could stand it no longer. He jumped out of the car and ran over to the man.

"David?" he asked, breathlessly.

"Yes," the man replied, looking up in bewilderment at his inquisitor. But it was more of a statement than a question.

## 2

The thousands of Watchmen who crowded the Civic Center stared in bewilderment as Bruce Kline raced through his talk. The talk, once so important to him, now was simply keeping him from an urgent matter. He began skipping some paragraphs entirely, though he still took care to get all of the "sound bites" in.

"...The wisdom of the world is foolishness to Jehovah... Why waste your limited time on men's opinions when you can delight in Jehovah God's word? Studying philosophy is the same as cultivating bad associations; it 'spoils the useful habit' of associating with God's Word..."

He was only about halfway through the talk when out of the corner of his eye he caught sight of a white figure slowly moving towards him from stage left.

A murmur arose from the audience as people speculated as to who this man might be.

Bruce stopped in mid-sentence to look at the approaching figure. He had asked David to wait for him just off stage: personally dragging an old wooden chair onto the spot to drive home the point that he wanted him to sit still until the talk was over.

Evidently David had other ideas. As David slowly shuffled towards the podium, Bruce wondered what he should do. There had been a staged enactment in the morning that had featured actors in similar robes, so people probably thought this was another actor about to play a part in Bruce's talk.

But this was King David: the first man to be resurrected in modern times! It was a miracle that marked the start of Armageddon and the thousand-year reign of Christ and the anointed! Bruce was not about to stand in the way of this!

"Brothers and sisters!" Bruce shouted, raising both hands high above his head, and breaking into instant tears: "I give you King David, recently resurrected! This is for real! This is the moment we've all been waiting for!"

Bruce stepped back from the podium, turned towards David, and began to applaud.

There was no doubt in any of the thousands of Jehovah's Watchmen's minds in the audience. No speaker had ever raised his hands above his head or burst into genuine tears before. Much less a member of the anointed—much less a member of the Governing Body! This was real. This was it.

In a moment the majority were on their feet, some applauding wildly, some hugging each other, crying and laughing at the same time. Some dropped to their knees, praying and sobbing uncontrollably.    Several elderly women fainted outright.

David had reached the podium now, and surveyed the bedlam before him. He displayed a confident smile and bided his time for a full five minutes as he watched the utter pandemonium play out in front of him.

At last he motioned for them to settle down.    Seeing this, one of the stagehands rushed to the microphone and raised it to the level of David's mouth. He had to be over six and a half feet tall: dwarfing Bruce's five and a half foot stature.

Bruce wondered if David would know what a microphone was.   He hadn't seemed surprised by the ride in the rental car. What he mostly seemed was dazed and incoherent up till now.

The Watchmen were making a new commotion now: telling each other to be quiet and pay attention:

"He's going to speak!"

"Quiet sister, so we can hear!"

"Armageddon will start now, and he's gonna tell us what Jehovah wants his people to do."

Eventually the noise quieted down—except for one tall man who stood with his scrawny arms raised up over his head. His eyes were closed and his face pointed heavenward. He kept calling out: "Praise Jah!   Praise Jehovah! Praise Jah! Praise Jehovah!" He sounded like a broken record or a Hare Krishna with the wrong mantra.

David continued to smile and to wait for total silence. When it appeared that it would never come, Bruce stepped forward again.  The microphone was now way too high for him, so he craned his neck and projected into it.

"Brothers and sisters!    Jehovah's people are not a disorderly people. Jehovah needs your silence now! King David is about to speak!"

"Praise Jah! Praise Jehovah!" The skinny man's voice seemed to grow louder as the others fell completely silent.

"Brother, be quiet!" a rotund woman seated next to him ordered. She reached up and yanked on his belt, toppling him over across her lap.  From this unexpected and rather improper position, the man gazed up at her with a baffled look. But it seemed to knock the wind out of him and his trancelike praising. At last all was quiet.

"Brothers and sisters—for I hope you will allow me the privilege of calling you such," David began, and was greeted by another standing ovation, which he had to eventually motion into silence again.

No one seemed surprised that he spoke perfect English instead of Hebrew. Bruce smiled at the thought: Rutherford had been right about that too.

"Our dear brother here," David continued, with a graceful wave of his hand towards Bruce, "has stated that philosophy is a waste of time. But I would like to ask a question: what *is* philosophy? Isn't it from the Greek *philosophia*, meaning 'love of wisdom'? I tell you, my friends, the love of wisdom can never be a waste of time; the unexamined life is not worth living."

Bruce swallowed hard. The boys in Brooklyn weren't going to like this. But they had been wrong before and had learned to roll with the punches. Besides: it didn't matter anymore; they were no longer on their own, struggling to determine the meaning of God's Word: God had resurrected one of his best representatives to lead them!

"If there are words of a god that men can hear, would such words always be more valuable than what any man could ever say?" David paused and took a long look at the audience before him. He took a sip from the same glass of water Bruce had been drinking from, and then continued.

"I can tell you this: I heard the voice of a god during my lifetime, and it often prevented me from doing things that would've led to my harm. Things that other men encouraged me to do. So, I ask you: which was better: the words of God or the words of men?"

'That's the ticket,' thought Bruce. 'He's coming around to our way of thinking now.'

"But, do you see the problem with the written or spoken word?" David waited as if he was expecting someone to answer. When no one dared to speak up, he continued: "If I hear a voice inside my head I know it's from God (unless I've gone mad), but if I hear your words telling me that you've heard the word of God, or you hear my words telling you that I've heard the word of God— there is no reason for us to believe one another. Because now it has been filtered through the words of men again. A chain, after all, is only as strong as its weakest link.

"So, if you point to a book—as our brother Bruce has done repeatedly today—and your human words say "This is the word of God" then we are stuck relying on the words of men to tell us what are the words of God—and we already agreed that the words of men are not a trustworthy guide."

He looked around as if expecting someone to challenge his statement, but all he got were confused looks. This isn't what they were expecting to hear.

Bruce began to perspire.

"Brother – er King David? Can I ask you a question?" It was the rotund woman. With the skinny man now safely off of her lap, she jumped to her feet and waved her hand in the air as if she were in a classroom with a burning question for her teacher.

"Yes."

"What was it like to die and then come back to life?"

Several people applauded the question; this is the sort of thing they wanted to hear about.

"Well," David replied, measuring his words out slowly, "just prior to death I had some considerable pain, but death itself was *nothing*. And today, well, I just seem to have awoken from a long sleep."

"What was it like to hear Jehovah's voice speaking to you?" another woman called out from the audience.

Several more questions sprang up from the crowd in rapid succession, some interrupting others:

"Is the preaching work over?"

"Has Armageddon begun?"

"Who will be resurrected next?"

Then a pause. David seemed to be mulling it over, deciding which question to tackle first, when Peter Frawley—a local journalist who was evidently covering the convention—rose to his feet.

"How do we know that this is King David back from the dead?" he asked.

Bruce stepped up to the microphone again. He wished now that David had stayed in the chair. "Brothers, sisters: this is not a question-and-answer free-for-all session." Bruce's voice was stern as he shouted into the microphone. "Jehovah's people humbly and patiently accept the meat in due season that is fed to them: they *don't* try to snatch it off the stove before it's ready to be served! They wait until it's placed on the banquet table and they are invited to partake."

A guilty silence settled over the crowd. Bruce cleared his throat and concluded: "I am taking King David to Bethel to meet with the Governing Body. After that we'll release an announcement to the congregations through the channel that Jehovah has provided and has used for over a hundred years: the Watchman Bible and Tract Society."

## 3

They met him at the airport, as Bruce knew they would: two members of the Governing Body in a sleek, chauffeured limousine.

It was brother Melvin Hershey and brother Andy Reese: the "candy-bar twins" as Bruce secretly referred to them: though they were anything but sweet. They were the youngest Governing Body members, though they had joined the club five years before Bruce. They had never stopped treating him as the new kid on the block, despite the fact that Bruce had now been a member of the Governing Body for a quarter of a century.

"This is ostentatious," he told them, pointing to the limo.

"Just in case your story proved to be true," Hershey replied.

"We didn't want to appear cheap," Reese laughed. He opened the door and motioned David inside, "Your majesty," he said with a bow.

Bruce felt like kicking him. The blatant skepticism was insulting. He'd just have to grin and bear it for now. He climbed in the back next to David. Hershey and Reese sat facing them.

The limo took off, and the candy-bar twins spent the first ten minutes of the ride from La Guardia to Brooklyn Heights smiling at David: trying their best to make him feel uncomfortable. But if they succeeded, David showed no signs of it.

It was Hershey who finally broke the silence. "Heard you made quite a stir at the San Diego convention."

"A real fiasco:" Reese chimed in, "you got Jehovah's people sounding like a convention of holy-rollers, from what I heard."

"Is not each man responsible for his own actions?" David asked.

"Of course," Hershey quickly replied, "but we *lead* our people."

"We tell them how to behave and what to expect," Reese added, "we always have; it's our responsibility as shepherds of Jehovah's people."

"As a former shepherd and king, I'm surprised that you wouldn't know that," Hershey said.

"Is it possible, do you think," David asked in reply, "to assume more responsibility than any man has a right to claim?"

"The responsibility of a leader *is* awesome," Hershey responded.

"And one of our responsibilities is to ensure that no one else leads Jehovah's people astray," Reese added with an accusing look.

"Yes, we like to take care of the 'leading astray' *ourselves*," Bruce couldn't help but add with a sarcastic laugh.

# 4

Bruce took David to his room to freshen up before meeting the rest of the Governing Body. Standing in front of his closet, Bruce eyed his wardrobe, and then looked up at the height of the man beside him. He smiled and shook his head; nothing he had would fit the man. Besides, the psychological effect of the white robe might work in their favor.

They had lost three hours with the time difference. It was nine-thirty at night here in Brooklyn, even though Bruce's body felt that it was only six-thirty. The Governing Body never met this late in the evening except in a major emergency. The fact that they had called a ten o'clock meeting was telling; it either meant that they were acknowledging the resurrection of David, or that Bruce was in big trouble.

He splashed some water on his face, stared into the mirror, and began mentally rehearsing what he might say at the meeting. Before he got very far, however, his thoughts were interrupted by a strange noise. It sounded like a motorcycle, having lost its muffler, had driven into his room, and had begun slowly and rhythmically revving its engine.

Bruce grabbed a hand towel and rushed out of the bathroom to see what the matter was. There, on his bed lay David, curled up in a fetal position and snoring for all he was worth.

"Big man, big snore," Bruce said with a shrug. He wasn't about to wake him. He headed to the meeting alone, still wondering what he was going to say.

As he entered the brightly lit conference room he saw all the other members were already present: each seated in their regular spots around the large oval conference table. Judging from the dried coffee spills on the papers spread out around brother Henderson's cup, it looked as if they had already been discussing the matter for some time.

"Sit down, Bruce," Henderson said, with a wave of his hand that toppled the cup over and spilled what little coffee remained.

Bruce sat down and studied the eyes of the eleven men who had stopped talking and now were intently staring at him. From what he read in those eyes it looked like it was going to be a long, rough night.

"So, tell us what's been going on," Henderson said in a stern voice, as he mopped up the spilled coffee with large paper-towels. "Or are we to be the last to hear of announcements made to Jehovah's people?"

Bruce now knew for sure that he was joining a meeting already in progress; brother Henderson would never forget to start a meeting with a prayer. In fact, he would often use the prayer as an introduction to the agenda: if there was someone who needed to be taken to task, for instance, then Jehovah would first be asked to "guide the erring brother" and to "bring him back into harmony with the organization." It was a great way to fully state the accusations while forcing the accused to listen quietly with head bowed.

"I'm sorry; brothers," Bruce began, "I tried to keep it quiet till I got him here, but he wandered onto the podium, and I wasn't about to stifle Jehovah's anointed."

At this point brother Hershey turned to brother Reese and said, "Do you want to tell him, or should I?"

"While we were awaiting your arrival," Reese replied, looking with disdain at Bruce, "we concluded that this man you have introduced is *not* King David back from the dead."

"How did you conclude that?" Bruce asked in mock astonishment, though he knew the answer all too well.

"You should know the answer to that," Hershey snapped. "The resurrection doesn't start before Armageddon."

"We used to think it did," Bruce reminded them. "Brother Rutherford—"

"That's old light!" Reese shouted, as if Bruce had mentioned something glaringly offensive and inappropriate.

"We've gone back to old light before," Bruce reminded them.

"Give me one instance where we've gone back to old light!" Hershey demanded.

"I can think of several," Henderson calmly responded. Being chairman of the Governing Body had its advantages: everyone became quiet and gave him their attention.

"We're not going to argue about old light versus new light," he continued. "That's not relevant. We have always changed our views in harmony with the facts. Rutherford himself did that: when he saw the Great Crowd coming in he changed the long-held view that they were a Heavenly class to their being an Earthly class. He *had* to; there were more than 144,000 of them," he chuckled, "and Revelation says only that only that number—that *sealed* number are in heaven.

"So, if King David shows up on our doorstep one fine morning, we're not going to argue with Jehovah about his plan. No, we're going to adjust our view and accept the new light—even if it happens to match what we thought was older light."

Having laid down the law on that topic, Henderson looked longingly at his empty coffee-cup, sighed, and then turned to address Bruce directly.

"Now, *you* have acted irresponsibly—but that's the least of our concerns right now. You have raised certain expectations amongst Jehovah's people. So now we must discuss 'damage control'."

"Can't we just ignore it and hope it goes away?" Cyril Fenders suggested hopefully. He was the closest thing Bruce had to a friend,

"That's ridiculous!" Reese said in a dismissive tone.

"I think we at least have to publicly reprove brother Kline," Hershey added.

"Now, wait a minute," Bruce said, "You haven't heard my side of it, nor have you even taken a look at the man."

"We don't need to," several of the brothers said more or less in unison.

"You don't *need* to?" Bruce exclaimed. "You know who you remind me of right now?"

"Do tell," Hershey said with feigned indifference.

"The Catholics!" Bruce cried, slapping the tabletop with the palm of his hand.

All mouths fell open; none of them had ever been accused of acting like their archenemies before.

Even Cyril took offence: "Would you care to explain that remark?" he asked.

"With Galileo," Bruce explained. "Remember how they wouldn't look through his telescope? They thought they had all the answers already. The Earth couldn't possibly revolve around the Sun! They had determined that from their misinterpretation of the Scriptures, and they didn't need to see the physical evidence that contradicted it because they knew it couldn't *possibly* contradict it.

"Well, the truth is, brothers, the physical evidence *did* contradict their idea, and they are held up to ridicule to this day for their stubborn refusal to even consider it.

"Now look at us: back in the twenties our Society purchased Beth-Sarim as the House of the Princes. We fully expected that Jehovah would resurrect the Ancient Worthies on that spot, or bring them there, and that they would live there while directing the work and guiding us."

"Well, in 1925—" brother Klaus began: he was the oldest member and the only one still alive who had actually served at Bethel in 1925.

"Yes, yes," Henderson interrupted, "we know: Rutherford made an ass of himself by insisting the resurrection would begin in 1925. He was wrong about that date. But even after 1925 he still held to the belief that the Ancient Worthies would be resurrected, after which Armageddon would begin. In fact it was after 1925 when he bought Beth-Sarim and made the deed out to King David, Abraham, and the other Ancient Worthies."

"He died believing that," Klaus added, sadly shaking his head.

"Yes," Bruce agreed, "and it was only years after his death that the Society sold Beth-Sarim and abandoned that idea.

"But, the other day I was at Beth-Sarim, and there was King David knocking on the door in his white robe: resurrected from the dead! Rutherford was right: the resurrection happens at the *start* of Armageddon!"

"How do we know this isn't some homeless person?" Cyril asked, still sore about the "Catholic" insult.

"Or someone playing a prank?" Klaus asked. "You know that happened to Rutherford. Some hobo came up to him and said, 'Hello, Judge, I'm David! Give me the keys to my house!' But Rutherford didn't fall for it; he said David wouldn't be dressed like a tramp."

"That's true," Bruce agreed, "the homeless don't typically wear beautiful, spotless white robes, and they're not in perfect physical health. As for being a prank: no one knew I was going to Beth-Sarim today, so how could they have arranged it? No, brothers, this is the genuine article. All you have to do is take a look through the telescope to see it."

No one could think of an answer to this, and the men glanced at one another in silence for several tense seconds. The time had come for a verdict.

Bruce began to perspire as his heart raced.

At last Henderson cleared his throat and said, "Well, as long as you've seen fit to drag him clear across the country, let's at least have a look at him before we send him packing. Bring him in."

Bruce smiled sheepishly: "I'm afraid he's sleeping at the moment."

"Been dead for three-thousand years, and needs a snooze right now?" Klaus asked.

The men laughed a little. Then Henderson said, "Well, now we know that we'll still need sleep in the New Order.

"Tomorrow morning then. We'll get to the bottom of this first thing after breakfast."

**5**

Bruce spent the night on the futon in Cyril's room. He knew he would never get to sleep above David's snoring. But he found his own thoughts keeping him from sleep. What had he done? Had he really found King David? Was this the start of what they had all waited for their entire lives? Was the New Order here at last?

There were a million questions to ask. Why hadn't he asked David anything of consequence all day? "Because he kept falling asleep," he muttered in answer, causing Cyril to stir in the darkness a few feet away.

At 5 AM he could no longer stand his restlessness. He threw back the covers, grabbed his bathrobe, and headed down the hall to the common showers.

There was one young early-rising Bethelite emerging from one of the shower stalls. Somewhat embarrassed to come suddenly face to face with a Governing Body member, he stood there in his dripping nakedness at a loss for words or actions.

"Let me show you something," the young man said, having finally recovered his voice. He led Bruce over to a nearby shower-stall and thrust open the door. "Look at this! Isn't it disgusting?"

Bruce peered into the stall, half afraid of what he might see. To his relief it was just a potted palm tree standing under the shower nozzle as if patiently waiting for one of them to water it.

The young man searched Bruce's eyes for signs of disgust, but failed to find any. "It's a waste of precious water!" he explained, sounding surprised that it required an explanation. "I've seen this in here with the shower running for twenty minutes at a time! I've warned the brother who owns it. I told him to stop—unless of course he had permission from the Governing Body. But he's never given me a straight answer about that. So let me ask you: does he have permission, or is this a waste of water?"

So this is what it had come to, Bruce thought. He couldn't think what to say to this half-crazed brother, so he wordlessly escaped into a shower-stall.

Enjoying the sensation of the pinpricks of water against his body, he sighed to think that this was the only physical pleasure left to him. The sight of the brother's youthful nude body stuck in his mind, and he said a quick prayer to try to rid himself of it.

He indulged himself for several minutes. Then he pushed open the shower door and peered around: thankfully, other than the palm tree, he was now alone. He threw on his terrycloth bathrobe and sandals, and headed to his room.

He unlocked the door and opened it slowly so as not to awaken his guest, though he doubted that anything could be heard over the snoring. But he entered a silent, dark room. Making his way carefully past the bed he eased the window blinds open a crack, letting in just enough light to make out the surroundings. Glancing back at the bed he saw that it was empty. He quickly turned to the bathroom—it was empty as well.

The thought that immediately popped into his head was that it had all been a dream.

**6**

David had awoken at 4 AM, as was his custom. Finding himself in unfamiliar surroundings with no one to talk to, he had wandered out of Bruce's room, and after finding the Bethel library closed, he had wandered down to the lobby.

"Can I see your room key?" asked Sam, the young brother who was serving as the lobby guard.

"I don't know, *can* you?" David replied with a curious look. He didn't mean it sarcastically, but that's how Sam took it. He was new in this position, and hadn't yet earned anyone's respect.

"Do you have a room key or not?"

David held out his empty palms. "I have no pockets," he said. "I don't see a room key, and if you don't see a room key, I think we could safely agree that I have none."

Normally, Sam would assume that the man was being a smart aleck— probably an elder who felt put upon being questioned by a lowly ministerial servant. But the man was hard to read because he smiled and looked as if he was engaged in a pleasant conversation that he was genuinely enjoying.

"I'll have to ask you for your room number," he said, using his "official" tone of voice.

"Ah, are the rooms *numbered*? How clever."

"Look, is this a joke or what? You can't be wandering around the halls in your bathrobe at this hour. Do you belong here? Are you a Bethelite?"

"I don't believe so," David said, looking thoughtful. "Can you tell me what a Bethelite is?"

"Alright, you're outta here!" Sam yelled. "Now get out before I call the police!"

David looked hurt by the change in Sam's tone, and slowly walked down the few odd stairs that separated the lobby from the front door.

Then Sam remembered what his predecessor had told him about the gay men from the Hotel Margaret across the street: sometimes they would wander around in a confused state—"probably after taking drugs"—and on rare occasions they'd even come in here by mistake, thinking it was the hotel.

"Go back across the street where you belong!" Sam called after him. "There's no queers here!" he hoped the minor insult would keep the odd fellow from returning.

David walked across the street and into the lobby of the Hotel Margaret. There were always a few men sitting on the poorly upholstered chairs or milling around the well-worn pool table, and this time was no exception.

Danny was the resident pool shark: a short, wiry Latino who sported a goatee. He was the first to spot David: "Look what's coming in," Danny said, using his pool cue to give a poke in the ribs to Herb: an obese middle-aged man with a blotchy complexion. As was his custom, Herb was dressed in pink slippers and a lacy blue bathrobe that was even more frayed than the coffee-stained recliner to which he seemed permanently attached.

Herb looked up in dismay as the tall, white-robed figure glided past them.

"Up for a game, there hot-shot?" Danny asked.

"Splendid," David said, stopping in mid-stride. He smiled and said, "What did you have in mind?"

"How about a little eight-ball? Say for five bucks?"

"I have no money."

"Say," Herb piped up, having recovered from the shock. "That's a nice bathrobe. I don't think we've met. When did you move in?"

Before David could answer, he felt the floor shake and heard the distinct thud of a heavy suitcase being dropped behind him. Turning to look, he saw the unimposing figure of Peter Frawley standing there, out of breath, wiping his glasses, and looking surprised to see him.

Peter held out his hand and David reflexively shook it. "Peter Frawley, of the San Diego Reader. Pleased to meet you, uh—King David?"

"This dude's a king?" Danny asked in amazement.

"That's what I'm here to find out," Peter replied. "Can we sit down? I've been traveling all night: barely missing connections and waiting around airports. My editor doesn't believe in shelling out for direct flights (in fact it's rare that any of his reporters ever get out of town). I only just arrived: I haven't even gotten a room yet."

"Well, listen, Scout," Danny said, having chosen a nickname that seemed to fit Peter while sounding condescending and vaguely derogatory at the same time. "Go get a room, and catch some shut-eye and we'll keep your king friend here entertained." He was already dreaming of the sizeable amount of money he could hustle out of a king.

"Okay," Peter agreed with some hesitation. Then, pulling closer to David and speaking more softly, he added: "I'll just get a room, and then we can talk in private. In the meantime please don't go anywhere! I just traveled clear across the country to interview you!"

Peter hoisted up his suitcase and lugged it around the corner to the registration desk. When he had disappeared, Danny began chalking up his pool cue. "Okay, it's you and me, your Excellency. I'll even spot you for the fiver."

"Oh, for God's sake, leave him alone, Danny," Herb demanded. "You don't have to hustle everyone, do you? I want to talk to this guy! We haven't seen a new face in here for months."

Herb knocked several days' growth of newspapers off the chair next to him and patted on the newly revealed cigarette-burned cushion: "Here, sit yourself down," he said to David with a smile.

David smiled back and sat down.

"My name's Herb, and I just broke up with my partner three weeks ago: I'm available and on the rebound, so I'm easy right now. But you don't look like the type of guy who'd take advantage." He batted his long false eyelashes in an attempt at flirtation.

David seemed to be at a loss for words.

"You wanna come see my room?" Herb asked hopefully.

"Oh geez!" Danny exclaimed in exaggerated disgust as he racked up the pool balls. "Why don't you queers go play with yourselves."

"Takes one to know one," Herb said in a singsong voice, keeping his eyes glued on David.

"And when you get tired," Danny continued, "(which in Herb's case won't be long) come back and play a real man's game."

"What is a 'real man'? " David asked.

Danny and Herb eyed each other, to see if either of them had figured this guy out yet. But both returned only perplexed looks.

"You look like a real man to me," Herb said, turning his gaze back to David and giving him an exaggerated wink.

"Hey look," Danny said, seriously at last, "if you want to know what a real man is, forget that faggot and come up to *my* room."

"Thank, you," David replied, "but I'd prefer to discuss it here in an open forum."

"What's the matter, don't you like us? We're not good enough for you or somthin'?" Danny asked angrily.

"Oh, my!" Herb cried, "Maybe he's not gay!"

"Walkin' around in *here* with *that* outfit?" Danny remarked.

"Oddly enough, scholars aren't sure," David said. "In the Symposium Alcibiades related that he had lain with me all night and complained that I never touched him. In my time and culture, of course, homosexuality was commonly accepted. It wasn't a matter of morality, but rather of exercising self control; I practiced moderation in all things."

"You are freakin' me out," Danny said. "Why do you talk about yourself like you're dead or somthin'?"

"Well, you know, I had one of the most famous deaths in history." He paused and smiled while the other men in the room gathered around to stare at him with a mixture of fright and curiosity.

"But I don't want to talk about me. I want to talk about our definition of Man. What does it mean to be a man?"

"You gotta have a tool," one of the men offered. The others, including David laughed.

"Yes, but is that all there is to it?" David asked. "What about courage, temperance, self-control, compassion, passion, the search for beauty, truth, and wisdom?"

"We don't speak of such things," Herb said quietly.

"We must!" David cried, "if we be men."

"I don't have any self-control," Herb said. "If I did, my wife wouldn't have divorced me and I wouldn't have ended up in this hell-hole, living out my life like a zombie in constant search of bodies."

"I try to learn self-control," Perry, a skinny Jamaican man said in a weak voice. "I got to get off the crack, man; it messin' up my life. I can't even sleep no more like a normal person."

"How does a person learn self-control?" Another man asked. "Can anyone tell me that?"

"How does a man learn anything?" David asked.

"Through experience?" Someone offered.

"Yes, and do we gain experience from someone else, or is it something we do ourselves?" David asked.

"We do it ourselves; it comes from living our lives," Danny said, taking a long drag on his cigarette.

"So now, this "crack," or whatever else has enslaved us: if we experience something bad from it (like not being able to sleep) then this experience teaches us to stop using it, does it not?"

"It *does*," Danny agreed, glaring at Perry as if he were incredibly stupid.

"But I imagine," David continued, "that there are other things about it that makes it appear desirable, and so one tends to forget the negative consequences and focuses on these other things. Then later you have regrets when you experience the down side: like not being able to sleep."

"That's right, man," Perry agreed, "and I don't have the willpower to resist."

"You mean, up till now you've *told* yourself that you are a person who lacks sufficient willpower." David said.

"What you mean, man?" Perry asked, intrigued.

"I mean that there is more to you than just what we see here in this room. There is the man we see, and then there is the man you picture yourself as being in your mind. You carry this image of yourself around with you, and you act as if that image were really you: you have certain expectations of it— including the expectation of failure in regards to self-control."

"But that's an *accurate* image of himself," Danny said as he lined up a trick shot on the pool table; "he *is* a failure: just like most of the losers around here."

"Does he think he's a failure because he *is* a failure—or is he a failure because he *thinks* he is?" David asked.

"The chicken or the egg?" An old voice said with a laugh.

"Let me tell you a little story," David began, "once there was a man who lived inside a dark cave, wedged between the rocks so that he could not turn around. He was trapped and all he could see were shadows on the cave wall, and he mistook these for reality. He thought that all there was in life were these flat images in black and white: nothing beyond two dimensions. And so, not being able to see himself, he concluded that he also was a mere shadow. He didn't realize that he was a man of three dimensions.

"Now the truth is, there really were no rocks at all trapping him. It was his own image of himself that held him captive. In reality he could've stood up, turned around, and headed out of that cave into the bright sunlight any time he wanted. But he thought he was a mere shadow of a man, and that's what kept him imprisoned.

"We must learn to know ourselves truly. That is the beginning of all wisdom. Men are not shadows, no matter how convinced they might be that they are. Every man in this room is capable of turning around and facing the sunlight. Men have done this, and you are men: not shadows. Let each act be an act of improvement. Let each day—"

"Ah, there you are!" Peter called from across the room. "Are you ready for your interview?"

## 7

Bruce walked up to the large oval table at the front of the Bethel dining room, and sat down in front of the only unclaimed place setting: between Cyril and brother Hershey. The Bright camera lights stabbed his eyes from every direction. The new Bethel brothers squirmed nervously in their seats across the table, mentally repeating their memorized comments on the *Yearbook* text for the day.

Brother Hershey poked him in the shoulder. "Where's his excellency? Is he going to eat with us mere mortals?"

"I don't think so," Bruce replied quietly.

"He's not still sleeping, I hope!" Cyril said.

Before Bruce could think of an evasive reply, brother Henderson began the morning prayer. After that they launched into the day's text. The old men were so engrossed in watching the new Bethelites stammer and sweat through the ordeal that Bruce had time to think of an excuse.

At last the cameras were shut off and the dining room began the familiar clanking roar of hundreds of men serving themselves.

After carefully buttering his toast, brother Reese pointed his knife in Bruce's direction and asked, "So where's your 'David'? His voice was so loud that all conversation and motion ceased around their table and the tables immediately in front of them.

"He's gone out," Bruce replied, intently slicing his sausages into mouth-sized segments.

Brother Henderson gave Bruce a concerned look. "Didn't you inform him of our meeting with him?"

"Actually, no; I didn't get the chance. He had gone out before I got up this morning." He was careful to say "gone out" rather than "left"; he wanted to give the impression that David had merely stepped out and could be expected back at any moment.

"Look," Reese began, pointing his knife again, "we've bent over backwards to accommodate you and give you every benefit of the doubt. But if this man can't even show up for a meeting—a meeting with the *Governing Body* no less—then I consider the matter closed. We have no more time to waste on this."

"But I think," Hershey said, "that we need to devote some time to the little matter of indiscretion: conduct unbecoming a Governing Body member."

"We'll discuss this after breakfast," brother Henderson snapped.

The rest of the meal was observed in a pocket of silence surrounded by the clamor of hungry brothers oblivious to the altercation that had occurred at the head table.

Bruce left the dining room without waiting for the closing prayer. He went straight to the lobby. "Did you see a tall man in a white robe go out these doors early this morning?" he asked the young Bethelite manning the guard's desk.

"No, I would've remembered someone like that," came the reply. "But then, I didn't come on until 6 am. How early did he leave?"

"Where's the brother who was on the night-shift?"

"Gone on return-visits to Harlem, I'm afraid."

"Damn." Bruce shouted and left without even waiting to see the shocked look on the brother's face.

He went back to his room again just in case, by some miracle, David had reappeared there. But all he saw was an empty room with no evidence that anyone beside himself had ever been there.

Brother Henderson had already begun the meeting's opening prayer when Bruce arrived in the conference room. A semicircle of bowed, bald and balding heads greeted him. He sat down quietly next to Cyril, and tried to concentrate on Henderson's words.

"...to keep your house clean, even when it is one of our highest placed leaders, entrusted with extra responsibility and accountability to you, dear Jehovah. Help us to never run ahead of the vision or grow impatient at your divine timetable, as he has done. Help us rather to labor patiently in your service guided by the light you provide to your organization on earth. Give us an extra portion of your spirit to help us make the right and hard decision to chastise a brother in need of reproof: to guide this erring brother and bring him back into harmony with your organization. And we ask this all in Jesus' name. Amen"

The other men, including Bruce, echoed the "Amen." Then they all turned their attention to chairman Henderson.

"As you know," he began, "we have a painful duty to perform today. One of us has acted rashly and irresponsibly, marring our reputation for being faithful and above all discreet."

"That's putting it mildly," brother Hershey commented.

"Why don't you take the vote right now?" Bruce asked in a steady voice, though his chin quivered. "We all know the Scriptures on this issue, all of us having presided over our share of disfellowshipping cases."

Brother Reese leaned over to brother Hershey and muttered loud enough for all to hear, "It might sound different though, hearing it from the other side of the table for a change."

A few of the men chuckled at this, but the rest felt it too mean to even acknowledge with a polite smile.

"Very well," Henderson agreed, ignoring Reese. He closed the Bible he'd book-marked with Post-it flags at all the passages relating to disfellowshipping. It was, in fact, his "disfellowshipping Bible;" used only for that purpose. He had cross-references and notes hand-written in the margins so that he could deliver the "presentation" without much thought. He had a shelf full of Bibles back in his room, each one carefully prepared in this way for a distinct purpose, and clearly labeled on the spine with a felt-tip pen: "Weddings", "Field Service", "Return Visits", and so on. This particular Bible had been more discreetly marked with a simple red "D".

They sat for a moment unsure of how to begin without citing Scripture.

"Wait," Cyril spoke up at last. "There is an order of business I'd like to put first. One that may have some bearing on the case before us."

"Oh, can't it wait, Cyril?" Reese said as he rolled his eyes.

"No, it can't." Cyril insisted.

"Very well," Henderson said, "let's hear what you have to say. But it better have a bearing on the case before us."

"As you know," Cyril began, "our rate of increase has been falling for a very long time. Years ago we were the fastest growing religion: today false religions are growing faster. Meanwhile the rate at which members are leaving continues to climb at an alarming rate."

"And we're about to lose one more," this time the interruption came from Hershey, ostensibly in an aside to Reese.

"Brothers, please!" Cyril exclaimed.

"Alright," Henderson said sternly, "let's have a little order here. Brother Cyril has the floor."

"So why doesn't he tell us something we don't already know?" Reese asked with a long-suffering sigh.

"I'm getting to that," Cyril replied matter-of-factly. "I just received the numbers from the San Diego convention." He paused for a long sip of coffee.

"So, how did we do? Any new baptisms?" brother Klaus asked.

In their heyday, a hundred baptisms per convention was not unheard of, but these days they were happy whenever they got more than a half-dozen.

"Ten had been scheduled," Cyril paused again, scrutinizing his notes. At last he looked up, removed his glasses, and smiled. "My dear brothers, they had four-hundred and twenty-seven baptisms, praise Jah!"

The men stared at him in collective amazement.

"But that's not all," Cyril continued, "They sold out all of the literature, and started five-hundred and thirty-two new Bible studies! And when I checked the website this morning I found we had almost two hundred thousand new hits since Sunday! And I hear the emails have been pouring in as well in unprecedented numbers."

"This is surely a turning point," brother Klaus said thoughtfully. "But I don't see what it has to do with our judicial hearing on brother Kline."

They all turned to brother Klaus with looks of wonder. Didn't he get it?

Since Cyril still had the floor he took it upon himself to enlighten him. "What do you suppose all of those emails are asking, brother? They want to know where *David* is and what message he has for us.

"We held that same convention in major cities all across the world with little to show for it. The only thing different in San Diego was brother Kline's introduction of King David back from the dead. It has awoken the sleeping masses! The inactive and disassociated are flocking back to the Kingdom Halls. People who have been studying off and on half-heartedly for years are now diving headlong into our baptismal pools! This has energized them all!"

"Well, that's what I want to know too," brother Klaus replied. Slightly embarrassed at having appeared so dim, he sought to shift their attention. "Where *is* King David, and what does he have to tell us?"

"Find him," Henderson said, looking intently at Bruce, "and bring him to us straightaway." Then he stood up, and without looking at anyone added, "This hearing is postponed until further notice."

They all filed silently out of the room, leaving Bruce to contemplate his next move alone in the silence they left behind. As in all such cases, he began to pray earnestly. "Dear Jehovah, please bring this man back to me, whether he be your servant or not—"

He was interrupted by a knocking on the open door. "Excuse me, brother Kline?" It was sister Lois, the Governing Body's administrative secretary. He looked up at her but said nothing. There she stood, representing his normal life as if nothing life-changing had just occurred.

He felt as Dostoyevsky must've felt after waiting in line for the firing squad only to find himself—after a last minute reprieve—still very much alive and still very much threatened.

The familiar took on an overriding sense of being inconsequential while continuing in its ignorant self-importance. He almost laughed.

"Yes, Lois," he said wearily, "what is it?"

"A gentleman here to see you."

The fact that she said "gentleman" instead of "brother" meant that it was a worldly person. But Bruce didn't recall any such appointments. He was about to ask her to send the man away when she added, "He says it's in regard to a missing person, and that you'd know what he was talking about."

"Very well, send him in."

A short, thin, bespectacled man duly appeared in the doorway. Bruce motioned for him to sit down across the table from him. But the man, after closing the conference room door, took a seat right next to Bruce. He leaned forward and stared into Bruce's eyes as he spoke.

"I'm Peter Frawley, a reporter for the *San Diego Reader*. I was doing a feature story on your convention when I saw you introduce King David." He paused to let this sink in.

"Yes?" Bruce replied, trying to hide his impatience to hear what this man might know about David's whereabouts.

"I think we can help each other."

"Go on."

"I want exclusive rights to this story. I want to act as your press agent for all matters relating to King David."

"Is that your helping *me* or my helping *you*?" Bruce asked in feigned guilelessness.

"It's both. You're going to have a media circus here any minute: a reporters' feeding frenzy. Left to their own ends they'll make a laughing stock of your organization. As your press secretary I can go a long way towards keeping them under some control."

"We have our own media specialists," Bruce told him. "I'm sure they can handle it, and present our viewpoint more accurately than an outsider could."

"I'm not an outsider," Peter confessed, "I'm one of those inactive Watchmen who just got rededicated at the convention following King David's appearance. I was brought up in the truth—strayed for a while—and now I'm back. King David's appearance did that for me, and I'd like to help others like me by publicizing his presence."

"Well, I can bring it up at our next meeting," Bruce replied with a forced yawn. "It isn't solely up to me, you know."

"But you mentioned something about a missing person to my secretary. What was that all about?"

"I can deliver him to you," Peter said. "Just give me your word—one brother to another—regarding my status as press secretary to King David and I'll have him here within the hour."

"What will you report about him?" Bruce asked, thrusting his trembling hands into his pockets.

Peter stood up, smiled, and replied, "The truth, of course!"

**8**

The meeting started promptly at 1:00: immediately after lunch. Each member had blocked off the entire afternoon right up until dinnertime for this meeting. They were prepared to meet again after dinner if necessary, having arranged for other responsible elders to take their places as Book Study Conductors that evening.

Brother Henderson sat in his usual spot at the head of the table, with the others on either side. But, despite their best intentions, other matters of business occupied the first two hours, and it wasn't until 3:00 that David was sent for.

When David came into the room, he walked all the way around the table to the chair left empty for him at the furthest end: opposite Henderson. But he remained standing. The light streaming in through the windows behind him made his white tunic appear to glow and formed an aura around his head reminiscent of a halo.

"Won't you sit down?" Henderson offered, somewhat unnerved by the effect of the light.

"No thank you, I am unused to these chairs. I prefer to recline, or stand."

Several of the members made a written note of this. They had often seen illustrations in their own publications of the people of ancient times reclining around a table rather than sitting. It wasn't of great significance, but a decidedly good answer nonetheless.

"David," Hershey began, "we'll start with an easy question: can you tell me the name of your father?"

"Jesse."

"Good," Hershey said, "and of your mother?"

It was a trick question, as all the members well knew; the Bible did not record the name of David's mother. A fake would be at a loss to answer the question and would likely hesitate as he made up an answer.

"Phaenarete, the midwife," David answered without missing a beat.

"Can you spell that?" brother Klaus asked.

"Of course," David replied.

"Does the name Amasa mean anything to you?" Reese asked, with brother Klaus's pen still poised expectantly in the air.

"Amasa is one of my nephews: my younger sister Abigail's son."

Though not well known, this was knowledge easily obtained, and no one bothered to make a note. If he was a fake, it was apparent that at least he'd done his homework.

Reese stood up, walked behind David, and shut the Venetian blinds, plunging the room into semi-darkness except for a single shaft of sunlight emerging through a missing slat in the blind. The sunbeam was at the level of David's head and continued to produce the halo effect.

Henderson flicked on the ceiling lights but one of the fluorescents popped like a flashbulb which must've tripped a circuit breaker, and they were plunged into semi-darkness again: the only light coming from David's "halo".

"Please continue with your questions, brothers," Henderson requested, giving up on the lighting situation.

"Can you tell me," Cyril asked, "in what year Israel made you king?"

It was another trick question; David would have no idea that this occurred somewhere after the year we now call 1077 BCE (when *Judah*, not Israel declared David king). People of that time had no idea, of course, that we would date them backwards from a point in time that was in their future. But a fake David might easily fall for it and give this very answer.

"Israel did not make me king," David replied with indignation, "*Jehovah* made me king!"

It was spoken like a true king, and took them all by surprise.

They were all silent for a while, feeling suddenly ashamed of their petty questions. Finally brother Klaus's curiosity got the better of him and he asked, "Tell us, King David, what was it like to kill that giant Goliath?"

"Goliath?" David responded in surprise. "I never killed Goliath; that was Elhanan, the son of Jaare-oregim, of Bethlehem: he killed Goliath in one of our battles against the Philistines at Gob. I was almost killed in that battle by another giant by the name of Ishbi-benob. But Abishai the son of Zeruiah delivered me by slaying him."

The members seemed thunderstruck at this reply, and an even longer silence followed.

"Brother Kline," Henderson said at last, "will you kindly escort King David from the room for a moment?"

Bruce stood up and opened the conference room door for David, who dutifully followed him out into the lobby where an anxious Peter Frawley was waiting.

Henderson waited for Bruce to return, and then he slowly surveyed the faces he knew so well.

"This is King David," he pronounced. "No man pretending to be David would ever deny the most famous story told about him."

"But he's contradicting the Bible's account," brother Klaus complained.

"Well," Cyril explained, "many bible scholars have held that the account at Second Samuel 21:15-22 is the true account of how Goliath was killed by *Elhanan*, not David, and that it later became attributed to the much better known David (as legends always eventually become attached to great men's names).

"In fact verse 22 is a foreshadowing of that very process: despite relating how four giants (Goliath among them) were killed by David's men (with David not participating in the battle after having fainted) it says they were killed 'by the hand of David, and by the hand of his servants.' Likely the part about 'his servants' eventually faded from the story and it came to be attributed to David alone, though he clearly had no part in the killing of the giants according to Second Samuel."

"But that contradicts the Bible's account in First Samuel 17 which relates that David slew Goliath all by himself," brother Klaus reminded them.

"Well, one of those stories must have it wrong," Henderson said, "and who but the real King David would know which one? I ask again: Who but the real King David would deny killing Goliath?"

"But the Bible contains no contradictions," brother Klaus insisted.

"No, of course not," Cyril agreed, "not in the original. But some minor corruption has set in over the course of the years and the many translations. We've always known there was this discrepancy, but of course we've never advertised the fact."

"Who knows whether Jehovah didn't arrange this 'discrepancy' for the sole purpose of revealing his anointed to us today?" Henderson asked. "Who else but we, seated in this room, would understand such a subtle sign?

"And when you combine this with the obvious sign of so many of the straying sheep coming back into the fold... it only leads to one conclusion."

"But I thought the latest understanding was that the resurrection doesn't occur until after Armageddon," brother Klaus reminded them.

"So, we were wrong," Cyril replied. "Is that anything new? We used to think that Jehovah was going to resurrect the Ancient Worthies at the start of Armageddon or even right *before* Armageddon to help guide his name people. Well, we were evidently *right* back then; current events have *proven* us right! We just let doubt creep in when it didn't happen in the years we expected it to happen. But who will question Jehovah's timetable?"

Since no one was evidently prepared to question Jehovah's timetable, Henderson asked for a motion to be made.

Cyril stood up and said: "I move that this man be acknowledged and welcomed as King David, back from the dead, sent to us by Jehovah to guide us through Armageddon."

Brother Stingler, silent till now (but always ready to second any motion), stood and stated: "I second the motion."

"All in favor?"

All hands went up except for those of Klaus, Hershey, and Reese.

"We have a quorum," Henderson declared, "the motion is passed."

"But he didn't even know that David was made king in 1077 BCE," Klaus complained, causing everyone else to roll their eyes.

## 9

For the rest of the afternoon they discussed how best to relate the message to all of the Watchmen worldwide. The *Watchman* and *Arise!* had already been printed for the next four weeks. The *Watchman Ministry* wouldn't go out for another month. The convention season had just ended. All of these normal means seemed too slow. They were determined to let everyone know within the next day or two at the most.

The Web seemed the most logical solution. But in some parts of the world the brothers had no access to it, and for those that did many were reluctant to dial up for fear of apostate sites and porn.

"Maybe we should hold a press conference," brother Stingler suggested.

"Deliver the news by means of worldly agencies?" brother Klaus asked, astonished at the suggestion.

"It is up to *us* to feed the household of faith," several said at once.

"But Jehovah doesn't say what means we can or can't use to accomplish that," Bruce said. "Don't forget how Jehovah used Cyrus, a worldly king, to liberate his people.

"Or how we've used our Associate Member status with the U.N.," Cyril said, "the very Image of the Wild Beast, to further the spread of our word."

"Speaking of the worldly media," Henderson asked, "who is that reporter lurking around the lobby?"

"His name is Frawley," Bruce replied. "I've given him exclusive coverage of David in the worldly media."

"Sounds like brother Kline has exceeded his authority yet again," Hershey noted.

"Some people never learn," Reese said.

"Unless they're chastised for their wrongdoing," Hershey concluded.

"Are we back to a judicial hearing?" brother Klaus asked in a hopeful tone. He wanted to get back to something he understood.

"This Frawley is a baptized brother," Bruce explained. "He is an expert at handling the media, and he's been on this story from the start. He's evidently well known in media circles and won't be thought of as a front man for us."

He hoped this would be enough to satisfy them. He didn't want to admit that he'd lost David and had to bargain for his return.

"Brothers, let's stay focused on the matter at hand," Henderson said. "Brother Kline is no longer on probation.

"How do we get the message out to the brothers worldwide that the resurrection of the ancient worthies has begun?"

"Can this Frawley get the story 'on the wire'?" Cyril asked.

"We can ask him: shall I call him in?"

"What! Into a Governing Body meeting? Kline, what are you *thinking*?" Hershey asked indignantly.

"Look, here's what I propose," Cyril intervened, "Let's write up a statement, put it on the website *and* give it to brother Frawley. That's the first thing. Then we call in the Writing Committee and get them going on a series of *Watchman* articles."

"And we should place calls to all the branch offices around the world," Bruce added.

"Very well," Henderson agreed, "that should cover it.

"Now, it won't be difficult to introduce the matter, but what about the *message* of David? What will that be?"

"The brothers are already asking whether or not the preaching work is done." Cyril noted.

"Why would that be questioned *now*," Henderson demanded, "and why would David be the one to answer it instead of the leaders of Jehovah's organization?"

"Brothers," Bruce began with a sigh, "we're looking at this all wrong. We've been running the show up till now because it was just *us*, and we had no earthly help. But now Jehovah has sent us help. It's no longer up to us to dream up what David will say when he is resurrected; he *is* resurrected! Now we just need to open the door, call him in, and ask *him* what his message is."

"No outsider has ever been allowed to participate in a Governing Body meeting before," Reese reminded them.

"Would you have Jehovah's anointed wait outside while we decide what he should say?" Brother Klaus asked in disbelief.

"Perhaps we should make him an honorary Governing Body member," brother Stingler suggested.

Hershey shot to his feet and proclaimed bombastically, "Spiritual Israel did not make me a Governing Body member: *Jehovah* did!"

The parody did not go totally unappreciated. Even Bruce had to smile; the levity was welcomed by most of the members.

"Brother Hershey," Klaus spoke with outrage in his voice, "are you making fun of Jehovah's anointed?"

"If you'll recall, Reese and I didn't raise our hands when that vote was taken."

"Skeptics in our midst," Klaus commented dryly.

"Come to think of it, you didn't raise your hand either," Reese reminded Klaus.

"No, but we had a quorum," Klaus replied, "so that's that, and I'm not going to show disrespect to Jehovah's anointed."

"Brother Klaus is right: the only thing that matters is that the vote passed," Henderson declared. "But maybe *you're* the one looking at this all wrong, brother Kline. The Bible doesn't specify what sort of help the ancient worthies are to provide us. Maybe they just join the ranks and start witnessing. Maybe David's chief use to us is as a figurehead."

"Another thing we need to address," Klaus said, "is the other Ancient Worthies about to be resurrected. If David appeared on the doorstep of Beth-Sarim, the others will too, no doubt. So, I move that we buy the place back. We don't want Abraham standing out in the street without a home."

"I've already been in contact with the current owner," Bruce said. "She's willing to sell for eight million."

"Eight million!" Henderson exclaimed in disbelief.

"It's not that far-fetched; housing costs are extremely high in San Diego these days," Bruce explained.

"I say we offer them three and see if they'll take it," Cyril said.

"Certainly; one never starts out offering the asking price," Henderson agreed. "Bruce, you may handle the negotiations since you've already had contact with the owner."

**10**

The following morning, as the Governing Body members were concocting David's message, Cyril, who had taken a break to check on his normal duties, burst into the room and flung a dozen copies of the *New York Times* on the table. "We've been scooped!" he proclaimed. "You'd better all stop what you're doing and read this."

---

**King David Back from the Dead?**
*Jehovah's Watchmen hail modern-day resurrection*

---

Several minutes of silence ensued as the men perused the article. Occasionally a "tsk-tsk" or "harrumph!" was heard, but generally there was silence until Henderson ventured his opinion that it was "mostly favorable."

"But the story has been leaked in the worldly press before we've had a chance to fully notify the brothers," Klaus complained.

"Well, we did put it on the website and called all the branch offices," Henderson reminded him.

"And just how does this Peter Frawley know what David's message is?" Reese asked.

"Well, I guess he interviewed him," Bruce replied.

"Why didn't *we* think of that?" Klaus asked, evidently forgetting that Bruce had suggested this the day before.

"Listen to this," Hershey said with evident disgust, "'David equivocated somewhat when asked why he had reported to the Jehovah's Watchmen upon his resurrection. "Maybe they need the most help," he replied.'"

"I see that as positive;" Henderson remarked, "that's exactly why he's here: to help us. After all, he's not about to help Christendom spread their false religion."

"'When asked if his resurrection heralded the end of the world," Reese read from the article, "'David quoted Jesus' words: 'of that day and hour no man knows.' And added that the Watchmen had made fools of themselves in the past by guessing at dates: something he intends to put a stop to.'"

"Just where does he get off saying he's going to put a stop to anything?" Hershey demanded.

"Oh, would you rather we *continued* making fools of ourselves?" Bruce asked with a chuckle.

"Here's the only part that really bothered me," Cyril said, "'Look for big changes in the leadership of the organization.'"

"Was that something David said, or something this Frawley character concluded on his own?" Henderson asked.

"That's not clear," Bruce replied. "And he could mean 'leadership' in the sense of *how* we lead, not necessarily *who* is leading."

"It's one and the same thing," Reese said.

"Of course it's not," Bruce argued.

"This article will be picked up on the wire across the country," Cyril remarked.

"Across the *world*," Reese corrected.

"Then it seems imperative to me," Bruce said, "that we get David in here and interview him ourselves. Then we write exactly what he has to say in the next *Watchman*."

"Maybe we should all just retire and go home and turn it all over to this charlatan," Hershey said angrily.

They all turned to brother Henderson for the final word.

"Listen, brothers, I am of the opinion that King David is a natural-born leader. Jehovah resurrected him first in order to help us to rally the troops. But he is primarily a figurehead. He can never be one of the anointed; having been born before Jesus' sacrificial death. So, he can't be of the remnant—can't be a Governing Body member. So, he can't make policy, and he certainly can't decide changes in 'leadership'."

A collective sigh of relief rose up around the table.

"But the brothers are interested in what he has to say," Henderson continued. "For many of them this is their first tangible experience with a supernatural event. They are curious: they want to know what death and resurrection are like. They want to know what King David thinks of the modern world, and more importantly what he thinks of God's organization on Earth today. This is where we want him to focus his attention. Not on doctrine or policy or leadership changes, but on energizing the brothers and attracting more people into Jehovah's organization before Armageddon shuts the door.

"So, yes, we should interview him, but only with these sorts of questions in mind.

"And I want pictures of him going door-to-door placing *Watchman* and *Arise!* magazines in householders' hands and reading to them from the *New World Translation*. That ought to shut our critics' mouths once and for all!"

"Look," Hershey spoke up, rising to his feet and beginning to pace, "everyone in this room knows that Reese and I have been against this idea from the start. But if you are all dead-set on this, then we ought to do it right. Has anyone bothered to ask him the 80 questions? Has he gone through the *Truth* book? Has he been baptized? Who knows what sorts of things he'll say to the press next time! Maybe he's some kook who believes in the Trinity and hell-fire for all we know!"

"Brother Kline acted irresponsibly," Reese added, "but now everyone else in this room is compounding it a hundred-fold. I agree with brother Hershey: we need to take stock. We need to find out what this 'David' believes before he starts representing the organization to the world."

"I took care of this already," Bruce replied. "I asked a Bethel brother— Jonathan Ingles—to conduct a Bible study with David."

"Well, that gets him out of our hair for about six months," Klaus chuckled.

"But maybe Jehovah put the knowledge of the truth in him when he resurrected him," Stingler mused.

"David did write prophecies about the Messiah, you know," Klaus added. "He knew more about the divine plan than anyone else during his lifetime. He had a special connection with God: having spoken with him on many occasions."

"Well, that should be easy to test," Hershey said with a gleam in his eye. "Let's get him in here and ask him the 80 questions."

"Oh, that takes too long;" Henderson said with a sigh, "let's just have this brother—uh—Jonathan?" Bruce nodded. "Let's have him administer the 80 questions today and find out how much he already knows, and report back to us."

## 11

"Question one: Who is the true God?" Jonathan asked David as they rode the subway towards Flatbush the following day.

"Jehovah is the true God," David replied in a monotone voice as he gazed out the window at the daylight flashing into and out of view.

"Question two: What kind of God is Jehovah?"

"A true one." David replied. "That was already established by the first question."

"Yes," Jonathan said, and then hesitated; not wanting to correct King David, "but that's not quite the answer they're looking for."

"If you already know the answers they're looking for, why are you asking me the questions?"

"It's a test to make sure you know the truth."

"What is truth?"

Jonathan knew that Jesus had remained silent when asked that question, and he wasn't about to presume to know more than Jesus.

"Hey, are you two Jehovahs?" a young black man, seated across the aisle, asked them. He had headphones on, and was holding the left speaker away from his ear in order to hear them.

"We are Jehovah's *Watchmen*," Jonathan replied, emphasizing the correction.

"Y'all know Jesus?"

"We know *of* Jesus, yes."

"I heard you don't believe in him, is that true?"

"No, it's not true. I can leave you with a publication—"

"And what do *you* believe, young man?" David asked.

"I believe that you Jehovahs are false prophets with a corrupt gospel. That's what my minister told me."

"And do you believe everything everyone tells you?"

"No. But he said y'all predicted the end of the world in 1925 and 1975, and then when it didn't happen y'all said you never said that."

"Is that true?" David asked Jonathan.

"It's not that simple," Jonathan replied. "But here's our stop."

They got up to go, but as they stepped off the train the young man called out to David, "He's leading you astray! You got to accept Jesus as your personal savior. Don't know *of* him, just accept him into your heart as the son of God!"

As they walked up the stairs to the street, Jonathan said, "There's a lot of people today like that who are misled by the world empire of false religion. They've been told that we don't believe in Jesus when of course we do, it's just that we don't believe in Christendom's pagan notion of a Trinity that holds that Jesus is God... Which leads me to question 6: Who is Jesus Christ, and what is his position in relation to Jehovah God?"

"You just answered that question," David replied.

"Yes, but do you understand that he was a descendant of yours? 'Son of David' was a title that he proudly bore."

"So I am told," David replied. "But that young man said that Jesus was *God's* son: not mine."

Jonathan realized that David was waiting for an explanation. "Yes, we believe that: Jesus is Jehovah God's son."

"But how can he be the "son of David" *and* the "son of God"? Did he have two fathers?"

"Not exactly. Jesus is God's son, but when he came to earth he had an earthly father: Joseph, who was your descendant."

"So this Joseph," David said after a thoughtful pause, "he acted like an *adoptive* father of this Jesus?"

"Sort of."

"But then, Jesus wasn't really a descendant of mine, was he?"

"Yes, he was."

"I'm sorry," David replied, "but this doesn't seem possible to me. If I were to travel to another land and some elderly man took me under his wing and called me his son, I might call him my "father" as an honorary title, or to show my affection and gratitude, but that could never make me a *descendant* of his."

"Well, look..." Jonathan said, hesitating as he struggled with how to explain it. "Jesus was a special case. He was born of a virgin—"

"What did you say?" David asked in astonishment.

"His mother was a virgin: Mary."

"The son of God has an earthly mother?"

"Yes."

"And she was a virgin?"

"Yes."

"Then what did Joseph have to do with it?"

"Well, nothing really."

"Then even if Joseph had been my descendant, *Jesus* certainly was not."

"But the Bible says he was."

"The Bible again, huh?" David said with a slight smirk. "That's the book you people keep referring to for all the answers, isn't it?"

"Yes; it's God's Word."

"How do you know that it is God's word?"

"Well, you should know;" Jonathan exclaimed, "you wrote a large part of it!"

"Me?" David asked, astonished once again. "Some people wrote down my dialogues, and probably made up their own in my name after I was dead. As for me: I never wrote a thing."

"You never wrote a thing?" Now it was Jonathan's turn to be astonished.

"No, I never wrote down a thing. I preferred to talk with people in order to seek the truth with them: just as you and I are doing today."

"But the Psalms! You didn't write any of them?"

"Not me."

"This is amazing."

"You see, you don't even know who the writers of this book were, and yet you trust it as your source of truth. That strikes me as irresponsible."

"Following the Bible is irresponsible?"

"Not necessarily 'following' it, but blindly trusting it as true when it is at odds with what we already know is true."

"But the Bible is not at odds with the truth; it *is* the truth."

"Well," David said with an intense look, "sit here on this bench with me for a moment and let's discuss truth."

"We really need to get to brother Conrad's house if we're going to go out in service today," Jonathan said as he remained standing. "And then I really wanted to visit sister Foley at the hospital before we head back to Bethel."

"Five minutes? A brief rest before we go on?" David pleaded.

"A 3,000 year old man does get tired, I suppose," Jonathan muttered, as he sat down.

"Now, tell me Jonathan: how many fathers did you have?"

"One," he said, chuckling at the ridiculous question.

"I also had just one father. And do you think that if we stopped and asked anyone on the street here they'd give us the same answer?"

"Of course."

"And if we went back in time to the first child born, do you think in all that time, in all those generations there would be a single instance of a man having more than one father?"

"No, I don't."

"Then, could we safely assume that part of the definition of a "man" is that he is a person who has just one father?"

"Yes, of course."

"And you say that Jesus was a man."

"When he was on Earth, yes."

"So, how many fathers did Jesus have?"

"One."

"And who was this one father of Jesus?"

"God."

"So Joseph was not his father?"

"No."

"Now, does the Bible say that Joseph was Jesus' father?"

"Well, no, not really."

"So, if Joseph was not his father, then he was not a descendant of mine."

"But Mary was."

"Does the Bible say that?"

"Well, no, not exactly. It's something we've surmised."

"Well, let me tell you something about my time," David said. "We were a patriarchal society. The bloodline was counted from the males. If my son had a son, that son was "a son of David." But if my daughter had a son, he was not called a son of David, but a son of his *paternal* ancestors. So, it wouldn't matter to anyone of my time whether Mary was the daughter of a descendant of mine; her son would not be considered a son of David, but a son of Joseph (but of course if Mary was a virgin, Jesus wasn't a son of Joseph either.)"

"Well," Jonathan replied hesitantly, "it's true that the Bible says that people had the *'opinion'* that Jesus was the son of Joseph: implying that this was only a common misconception."

David chuckled softly at Jonathan's unintended pun on the word "misconception."

"Yes, of course, according to the Bible's viewpoint, Joseph was not the father of Jesus," David agreed. "That was indeed a *misconception* in every sense of the word. But the only way people of the time would've understood the phrase "son of David" would've been that Jesus' father was a descendant in the paternal line from me. And so, calling Jesus "the son of David" within the context of my time is to say something at odds with what we know to be true."

"Yes, but today we know that a son is just as much a descendant of his mother as of his father. So, since Mary was a descendant of yours, the Bible is correct in calling Jesus the "son of David."

"But you already told me that the Bible does not explicitly state that Mary was a descendant of mine; that was just something you 'surmised'. In any case, the prophecies of my time concerning the Messiah were foretelling that he would be in my paternal line, and if "son of David" was a title applied to Jesus in Jesus' time, then it really only matters what that meant at my time and his time: not yours."

"Well, look, I guess it doesn't matter," Jonathan replied. "It only matters that Jesus was the son of God. Being the son of David was just to impress the people of that time, because they wouldn't have accepted him otherwise."

"So, what you're telling me is that it was a lie, but it was okay to tell this lie because it helped convince people that Jesus was the Messiah."

"Yes, that's right."

"Sort of a 'pious falsehood,' we might call it?"

"Yes."

"And tell, me does your organization, the Watchman, set this right today?"

"What do you mean, 'set it right'?" Jonathan asked.

"Does it set the record straight and tell people what you just told me: that Jesus wasn't really the son of David, and that this was just a pious falsehood?"

"Uh, no."

"So then it continues publishing this pious falsehood?"

"Well, yes."

"And whether a falsehood is pious or impious, is it still a falsehood?"

"Um—I'm not sure."

"Well, let's look at something else that might help us decide. Let's say I have a rotten apple and a wholesome one. Would we be correct in saying that the rotten apple was still an apple?"

"Yes, of course."

"Or if I had a lame horse and a fit horse, would they both still be horses?"

"Yes."

"So, the *attributes* of an object cannot change the *essence* of the object. And so we find—applying this rule to falsehoods—that it doesn't matter whether they are pious or impious: they are both still falsehoods."

"Agreed."

"And what sort of prophets publish falsehoods: true prophets or false prophets?"

"Well, uh—"

"Go ahead, speak the truth, my boy!"

"Well—"

"Would true prophets publish falsehoods?"

"Maybe sometimes, if it furthers their cause."

"And why do you suppose *false* prophets publish falsehoods?"

"To further *their* cause?"

"Exactly. So, now how would we distinguish between true and false prophets if both of them publish falsehoods in order to further their cause?"

"I guess we couldn't."

"You're right. So, let me ask you again: would true prophets publish falsehoods?"

"I guess not."

"Then, aren't we forced to conclude that the young gentleman on the bus was correct: the *Watchman* is a false prophet?"

Jonathan was at a loss. "Look, uh—" he stammered, "we really need to go."

"Very well, I'm rested now. Our conversation has refreshed me."

"It has only *confused* me," Jonathan confessed.

## 12

When they arrived at brother Conrad's house, all of the friends were standing about with concerned looks on their faces. None of them greeted Jonathan or David as they walked in. They were all staring intently at brother Conrad, who was speaking on the phone.

"What's going on?" Jonathan whispered to sister Conrad, but she only motioned for him to keep silent.

"Our prayers are with you, brother Foley," said brother Conrad, and he hung up the phone. He looked around at all of the eyes staring at him and announced, "he says she's dying right in front of him. The doctors say she won't last the night."

Jonathan appeared shocked by the news. "We were going to visit her after going out in service," he whispered.

"You'd better go right now."

"C'mon, David," Jonathan said, "I'll introduce you to everyone later. Sister Foley is very dear to me."

"Yes, by all means, let's go," David said.

The others stood around in disbelief until brother Conrad started a prayer. But David and Jonathan didn't wait to hear it: they bolted out the door.

They walked quickly back to the subway, and to Jonathan's surprise, David managed to keep up, and didn't seem out of breath.

On the subway Jonathan began telling David about sister Foley.

"She's been like a mother to me. My own mother is back in Ohio where I grew up, so I don't see her much living here in New York. Sister Foley picked up on how homesick I was and she and brother Foley used to invite me to their house every Sunday after the meeting. Until she started getting sick."

"She sounds like a very loving person."

"She really is. She'd make a nice meal, and afterwards brother Foley and I would study or sometimes play checkers, and she'd be there in the background, knitting and humming softly, or making us tea, or baking cookies." His voice cracked. "She always used to say when I'd have to go— she'd say: 'May each day in your life be a good day: may Jehovah always watch over you and keep you from harm.'

"Then she started getting sick. She had to have several operations over the past few years to remove tumors from her bladder. That caused her to miss a lot of meetings, and the elders counseled her on that. So she stopped going to see her doctor. She's been attending meetings regularly for quite some time now. But last week she passed out during the Theocratic Ministry School. The brothers called for an ambulance, and she's been in the hospital ever since. They said she was bleeding heavily and was severely anemic. But I had no idea it was this serious."

When they arrived at the hospital they saw brother Foley standing outside of her room crying. Jonathan embraced him. Then David stepped forward, took his right hand in both of his, looked into his eyes and said: "Our prayers are with you, brother Foley,"

Disengaging himself from David, brother Foley leaned himself against the wall. "The doctors can't seem to stop her bleeding," he told them as he wiped his eyes with a tissue. "They've been trying all week, but nothing works."

A doctor walked out of her room shaking his head. He glanced at the men in the hallway, then lowered his eyes and started to walk away.

"Isn't there anything you can do, doctor?" David asked.

The doctor turned around and stared at David with a hateful look. "Well, of course there is. As we've been trying to tell you all: she desperately needs blood."

"So, why don't you give her some?" David asked. Everyone appeared shocked by the question, so he added, rolling up the sleeve of his tunic: "She can have mine if you're short."

"And who are you?" The doctor asked, the hateful look replaced now with a look of hope.

"I am David."

"Pleased to meet you, I'm Dr. Weber. I've been looking after Mrs. Foley for the past few days. Tell me, are you a relative?"

"Alas, no."

"Look, David," Jonathan said, his patience nearly at an end, she won't accept blood; it's against God's law. It's question 48: What is God's law concerning blood? The answer is: Abstain from blood! Besides, we know there are alternatives to blood—"

"No, listen to me," Dr. Weber said: "The body's organs need a certain amount of oxygen to function. That oxygen is carried from the lungs by hemoglobin molecules in the red cells. We're currently giving Mrs. Foley supplemental oxygen through a mask, but there's little more we can do in that regard; she's already breathing virtually pure oxygen. The few red cells she has are fully loaded with oxygen, but her blood count is 9; that's so low that it can't adequately transport the oxygen her body needs. There's nothing more we can do except to give her blood: which would almost certainly save her life, even now.

"Mr. Foley, there is one last chance: you can sign a consent form to give her blood, or you can walk into that room right now and kiss your wife goodbye."

"What a cruel thing to say!" Jonathan shouted. "Get away from us and leave us alone!"

"You see how Satan tempts us?" Brother Foley asked David. But David knew it wasn't really a question, and remained silent.

The three men walked slowly into the room. Two nurses were standing beside sister Foley's bed, monitoring her. She had an oxygen mask strapped to her face, and she was gasping for air, breathing faster than seemed humanly possible. Hanging from the bed rail was a bag of bright red urine. One of the nurses laid a hand tenderly upon sister Foley's chest, trying in vain to ease the crushing pain there.

Sister Foley's eyes moved to Jonathan, but that was all the recognition she could offer: her entire being was caught up in the desperate struggle for air. All her body knew to do was to frantically pant, trusting the air to give her what was needed, as it had all of her life. But the action was pathetic since it was proving futile.

'Sometimes the body is smarter than the mind,' David thought to himself. 'It tries everything it knows to preserve life, while the mind throws the gift away.'

Dr. Weber came back in and studied the EKG. He frowned at the deep valleys that indicated a heart in pain.

Brother Foley sat down on the bed and buried his face in his hands, shaking the bed with his sobbing.

Jonathan began to pray aloud.

David watched the heart monitor as it traced each beat with a thin white line traveling up and down the pale green screen, accompanied by a beep barely audible over Jonathan's praying. David watched in hypnotic fascination for a few minutes when suddenly the peaks and valleys went flat and the machine emitted a high-pitched alarm.

The crash-cart burst into the room. A team of doctors and nurses ran in, shoved David and Jonathan out of the way, threw brother Foley off the bed and onto the floor in a heap, and began CPR. Dr. Weber called for epinephrine and atropine, which were quickly injected. Then he grabbed the paddles and yelled, "Clear!" Sister Foley jumped slightly in response to the electric jolt to her heart. The line on the monitor fluttered slightly, then went flat again. More CPR, more epinephrine and atropine, another electric jolt, more CPR...

The process was repeated continuously for an hour. At that point everyone had given up hope that her heart would ever beat again. Dr. Weber, wiping the sweat from his forehead, told the nurse to note the time. He stared at brother Foley, still lying in a sobbing heap on the floor. "I'm sorry," he said, and left.

"Brother, take heart," Jonathan said, kneeling down to his level; "look up at King David here; he is proof that there will be a resurrection."

Brother Foley slowly looked up to where David had been standing, but he was no longer there. He was now standing at the head of the bed with the palm of his hand placed gently on sister Foley's chest, as the nurse had done. He looked down at her and choked out the words: "May Jehovah always watch over you and keep you from harm."

**13**

Nearly a week passed in which David and Jonathan continued their discussions (when David wasn't engrossed in the Bethel library). Meanwhile the Governing Body took care of business, and scarcely thought about David.

But finally, they caught up with their business, and the subject turned, at last, to David.

"So how are the 80 questions going with David?" brother Hershey asked.

"Did you get any photos of him using the *New World Translation*?" brother Henderson asked impatiently.

"No, we didn't get any photos, yet," Bruce replied. "He's been going out in service and we didn't want to spook the householders by taking pictures of them."

"We'll stage something with a nice young couple from my congregation in an upscale neighborhood," Cyril offered.

"What about the 80 questions?" brother Reese said, echoing Hershey's ignored query.

"Jonathan went through them with him." Bruce replied.

"And?"

"He's really beyond such questions," Bruce sighed, knowing the answer wouldn't satisfy them.

"Did he know the answers," Henderson demanded, "or do we have to teach him?"

"It's not that simple," Bruce explained. "Every question he's asked seems to lead to more questions."

"Are we going to have more than 80 questions?" Klaus asked hopefully. "I never did think that was enough to ensure understanding."

"Look," Henderson said, "we're supposed to be the ones asking *him* the questions, not the other way around. If he has questions, then a study is in order."

"I'm afraid his type of questions wouldn't be answered by a Bible study."

"Nonsense!" Hershey remarked, "The Bible holds the answer to all questions."

"If Jehovah gave him knowledge of English, and how to get to Beth-Sarim, you'd think he'd give him a knowledge of the truth," Klaus commented.

Bruce hesitated a long time, sighed deeply, and said: "Maybe Jehovah gave him a more accurate knowledge of the truth than what we've been stumbling around in the half-darkness trying to make sense of."

"What are you suggesting now?" Reese asked.

"I think it's time we listened to Jehovah's messenger and found out what his message is," Bruce replied as calmly as he could.

"What does everyone else think?" Henderson asked, eyeing up Hershey and Reese.

"Oh, by all means!" Hershey exclaimed, "I'd love to take another crack at the charlatan. Brother Reese and I have some questions that will prove he's a fake. We've been waiting for a chance to interrogate him again in front of you all."

"I thought we'd gotten beyond that," Bruce commented.

"*You* have," Reese replied, "but some of us aren't so gullible."

"But we've already told the brothers—indeed the whole world—that David has come knocking at our door," Klaus reminded them. "How would it look now if we were to say he was a fake?"

"Let's not worry about that until we determine his legitimacy," Cyril advised.

"We already have," Henderson declared. "If we bring him in here it won't be to re-determine his legitimacy, but to find out if he has a message, and what it is." He looked into the eyes of all the men seated at the table to see if any dared contradict him. When he was certain that no one would speak he pressed the intercom button and said, "Lois, please send David in."

While they were waiting, Henderson strolled over to the window to gaze out, with his hands clasped behind his back. The other men knew he only did this when contemplating some major change.

David stepped in, nodded to the few who were looking his way, and then sat down in Henderson's chair at the head of the table. A few gasped at this, but Bruce and brother Hershey both smiled: each for his own reason.

"Er, brother Henderson," Cyril said softly, hating to disturb the man's thoughts, "David is here."

Henderson turned, and so did his expression. Deep creases formed between his eyebrows, and his face became flushed. But he took a deep breath and said nothing.

Hershey, still smiling, turned to David and asked: "Uh, David, if you're now seated comfortably in the chairman's chair, can you tell me who Adolph Hitler is?"

"Adolph Hitler?"

"Yes."

"No, is he a friend of yours?"

Bruce had to laugh at this, and a few of the other men chuckled as well.

"What are questions like *that* supposed to prove?" Henderson snapped.

Hershey ignored them all and continued his interrogation. "How about the Queen of Sheba?"

"Sorry, I haven't met her either."

"Are these some of the new 80 questions?" Klaus asked, bewildered.

"Where are you going with this, Hershey?" Henderson asked.

"I want to find out how much he knows about things that happened after David died."

"How could he know about such things?" Bruce asked.

"Good question," Reese replied. "You see, he's doing a good job of pretending not to know things that took place after David died, but then how does he know how to use a microphone, or an elevator? Why didn't he freak out in the car or on the plane? How can he speak perfect English when English hadn't been invented yet when he died?"

"Listen," Henderson replied, past all patience. "Jehovah taught him what he needs to know to help us with the preaching work in these last days. He evidently doesn't need to know the entire history of the world from the time he died till now in order to do that.

"Now, David: we'd like to know if you have any message from Jehovah."

"I do," David replied, standing to address them.

"Several days ago I witnessed a very tragic event. The death of one of our dear sisters: sister Foley."

"We're very sorry to hear that," Henderson replied, "but, of course, she'll be resurrected very soon into the New Order."

"Ever since witnessing that tragedy," David continued, evidently ignoring Henderson's comment, "I have been questioning young brother Jonathan, whom you appointed as my inquisitor and teacher. He also gave me some articles to read which I believe you gentlemen have overseen the writing of, and of course, I have been reading your book: the Bible."

"What is this in regards to?" Henderson asked.

"I want to remind you of a little story about myself from your Bible." David explained.

"The story goes like this: I was with my men, running from the jealousy of King Saul who was trying to kill me. We fled to the city of Nob, and we were exceedingly hungry. So what do you suppose I did? I went up to Ahimelech the priest and I lied to him, telling him that the king had sent me on an errand, and that he needed to feed my men and me. The priest believed my lie, but the only thing he had for us to eat was the sacred shewbread. Now, it was against Jehovah's Law for anyone but the priest to eat the shewbread, but we ate it that day."

With that, David sat down and waited for someone else to speak.

It was brother Klaus who spoke first: "You know, Jesus referred to that same incident in Mark 2:23-27 when he was accused of breaking the Sabbath." Shutting his eyes, he recalled the passage he had committed to memory from the *King James Bible* long before the *New World Translation* had even been thought of:

"And it came to pass, that he went through the corn fields on the Sabbath day; and his disciples began, as they went, to pluck the ears of corn. And the Pharisees said unto him, Behold, why do they on the Sabbath day that which is not lawful?
And he said unto them, Have ye never read what David did, when he had need, and was an hungred, he, and they that were with him? How he went into the house of God in the days of Abiathar the high priest, and did eat the shewbread, which is not lawful to eat but for the priests, and gave also to them which were with him? And he said unto them, The Sabbath was made for man, and not man for the Sabbath."

David smiled and nodded at brother Klaus, then he asked a surprising question: "Which of you men has children?"

"None of us have children," Henderson replied.

"I see," David said, and then lapsed into a thoughtful silence.

"Brother David," Henderson resumed.

"Yes?"

"What is your message to us from Jehovah?"

"I don't think the message is for *you*," David replied. "I think it is for your followers."

"Our followers?"

"Yes. People like sister Foley," David replied, standing back up.

"Just a moment," Henderson said, "if you have any message to communicate to Jehovah's people, you'll need to use Jehovah's channel of communication on Earth: the Watchman Bible and Tract Society. You can't just go off on your own! We all must hear and approve of the message first."

"Well," David replied, "whether you approve of the message or not, I must speak."

"Speak, then, David," Bruce gently prompted him.

"Very well," David agreed, "My message is this: blood transfusions are *not* against God's law. They *must* be used whenever they can help preserve life. Furthermore, it is the *duty* of every Jehovah's Watchman—indeed of *everyone*—to donate blood for this purpose."

A stunned silence followed.

Finally, David asked, "Will you publish this message from Jehovah in the *Watchman*?"

For some reason everyone turned to Bruce, as if he, being the one who introduced the "David problem" into their midst, had some sort of solution to this new dilemma.

So Bruce cleared his throat and slowly said, "David, look: we know how upset you are at witnessing the death of sister—that sister—"

"Foley," Cyril reminded him.

"Foley," Bruce repeated. "But the Bible is very clear on this point, and thanks to our critics, we've checked and double-checked its meaning constantly over many years. The command from Jehovah is to 'abstain from blood.' In order to follow God's law, then, Christians must abstain from blood transfusions. This law was in place before the Mosaic Law: it goes back to Noah's time, and so was not just for the Jews, and did not pass away with the Mosaic

Law. In fact, the Christian-Greek Scriptures restate the law as being in effect for Christians."

"I see," David replied. "But let me ask you this: was man made for the Sabbath, or was the Sabbath made for man?"

"The Sabbath was made for man," Hershey replied boldly: anxious to get into the conversation and bury David now that he had committed such radical heresy.

"And what do you suppose Jesus meant by that, in light of my little story?" David directed the question to Hershey, accepting the challenge in his eyes.

"He meant that the Sabbath law was put in place as a loving arrangement by Jehovah for man's good: to give him a much needed day of rest. But the Pharisees had turned it around into working a hardship on the people: applying it in such an overly strict sense that they thought Jesus' disciples had broken the law simply by plucking ears of corn to feed themselves when they were hungry."

"And he specifically mentioned my men eating the shewbread as also breaking the law?" David asked.

"Yes, he did."

"And today I'd like to add a third example," David said. "If we agree that Christians are to abstain from blood, and we agree that having a blood transfusion is breaking that law—"

"As it most certainly is," Henderson added.

"Then, what do you suppose Jesus would say if he had been there at the hospital the other day?" David asked. "Would he say: 'Good job, sister Foley: give up your life for the law! Remember, man was made for the law: not the law for man'?"

"Well, no. Of course he wouldn't say that," Klaus replied.

"Or, would he say something more like: 'Remember: the law was made for the good of man. It was not put in place to cause you hardship or to cost you your life. When strictly following the law of God to the letter would result in your death, then you must break the law.'"

A long silence followed.

"Gentlemen," David said, "I need your answer."

"Based on the Scriptures you quoted," Henderson admitted, "I can see where you might be led to such a conclusion."

"But the Bible clearly states that we must abstain from blood," Reese reminded them.

"Doesn't the Bible also clearly state that only the priest was allowed to eat the shewbread?" David asked, "And didn't Jesus explicitly state that it was, in fact 'unlawful' for me and my men to eat it?"

"Well, yes."

"And doesn't the Bible also clearly state that one must not do any work on the Sabbath?"

"Well, yes."

"And isn't there an example of God ordering the Israelites to execute a man for simply having picked up some sticks on the Sabbath?"

"Yes: in Numbers 15:32-36," Klaus answered.

"So, obviously when Jesus' disciples plucked ears of corn, their actions were breaking the Sabbath law as surely as if they had picked up sticks (an action which had merited execution by stoning on God's order.) So, in my case and in the case of Jesus' disciples, the law of God was broken, was it not?"

"Yes," the men murmured.

"These people broke the law of God in order to sustain their lives, did they not?"

"Yes," the men reluctantly agreed.

"So, sister Foley would've been acting on a Biblical principle if she had received a blood transfusion in order to stay alive." David concluded.

"Well, that's very clever reasoning," Henderson replied, "but you could use it, of course, to justify breaking any one of God's laws that you wanted. But, of course we know that the unlawful man will not find a place in God's Kingdom.

"And, whereas we know that the Sabbath Law and the laws concerning the priests and the shewbread all passed away; we know that the law given to Noah never passed away since it was given to all mankind, not just the Jews. And in the book of Acts we read that the Governing Body of Christians in the first century ruled that this law applied to Christians just as certainly as the law against fornication."

"Sister Foley did the right thing," Cyril added; "it was her Christian duty to obey the law forbidding blood transfusions, even if this test of her faith meant her life. All Christian Watchmen of Jehovah would've done the same thing."

"We can't just pick and choose which laws of God we'll obey," Reese added. "That's the hypocrite's and unbeliever's easy way out. If one of God's laws is a little inconvenient for them they ignore it. Just like Christendom comes up with its excuses for disobeying God's law about blood. But Jehovah's people are different. That's why we're his chosen people, and the ones who will survive Armageddon while all those outside of our organization will reap their just reward: destruction and death from Jehovah."

"But aren't you yourselves hypocrites?" David asked.

"No, we're not," Hershey replied in an exasperated voice as if he were dealing with a child.

"You stated that in your book of Acts, the first 'Governing Body' mentioned the law against blood together with the law against fornication," David observed.

"Yes: both equally important in Jehovah's eyes," Henderson replied.

"When this law was given to Noah," David continued, "wasn't there likewise another law given at the same time?"

"What do you mean?" Henderson asked.

"Wasn't there a law about being 'fruitful' and 'multiplying' and 'filling the Earth'?" David asked.

"Yes."

"Please tell me in what way you childless men have obeyed that law," David demanded.

Cyril spoke up: "That law was just for that time; the world had been emptied of people, and it was up to Noah and his sons to repopulate it."

"So, this law, given to Noah in the same breath as the prohibition against blood, is *not* in effect for us?"

"That's right," Klaus answered.

"But, you'll please excuse my ignorance," David said, "didn't you just tell me that we can't pick and choose which of God's laws we'll obey?"

"That only applies to the laws of God that are still in effect," Reese replied.

"So, let me get this straight in my head," David said. "God gave Noah two laws at the same time. One law was to not eat the blood of an animal, and the other law was to have as many children as possible. Am I right so far?"

"You are."

"But the one law is to be followed, because it is still in effect: and the other is not to be followed because it is no longer in effect. Am I right?"

"You're a good student, David," Hershey said condescendingly.

"Thank you, but then please instruct me some more on this issue. Please tell me *when* this law about having children ceased to be in force?"

The men were silent as they struggled for an answer.

"Uh—there wasn't any particular moment when this law passed away," Cyril admitted.

"What!" David cried in mock astonishment. "Do you mean to say that your Bible doesn't record God or one of his prophets ever saying that this law to be 'fruitful and multiply and fill the Earth' ever went out of effect?"

A long silence followed. Finally, Bruce spoke up: "No, there's no place in the Bible that says this law ever went away. But we know that the time is short, and raising a family is not the best use of our time."

"So, even though there is nothing in the Bible to indicate that this law ever passed away," David concluded, "you gentlemen have used your own reasoning to determine that the law is no longer appropriate for the circumstances of today. Is that correct?"

"Yes," brother Klaus said with a smile, relieved to have the thought spelled out so clearly.

"Well, then, gentlemen," David said, smiling himself. "Why can't we also use our own reasoning to determine that the law against blood is no longer appropriate for the circumstances of our day?"

"Well, I guess we *could*," Cyril offered, "except that it's already been determined for us by the apostles in the first century. In the book of Acts."

Brother Klaus shut his eyes again and recited: "'For it seemed good to the Holy Ghost, and to us, to lay upon you no greater burden than these necessary things; That ye abstain from meats offered to idols, and from blood, and from things strangled, and from fornication: from which if ye keep yourselves, ye shall do well. Fare ye well.' (Acts 15:28-29)"

Reese had been furiously turning pages in his Bible, and now added: "Conversely, on the issue of bearing children, Paul wrote:

"'Now concerning virgins I have no commandment of the Lord: yet I give my judgment, as one that hath obtained mercy of the Lord to be faithful. I suppose therefore that this is good for the present distress, I say, that it is good for a man so to be. Art thou bound unto a wife? seek not to be loosed. Art thou loosed from a wife? seek not a wife. But and if thou marry, thou hast not sinned; and if a virgin marry, she hath not sinned. Nevertheless such shall have trouble in the flesh: but I spare you. But this I say, brethren, the time is short: it remaineth, that both they that have wives be as though they had none' (1 Cor. 7:25-29)"

"So, then," David concluded, "it's not at all a matter of what God's law was to Noah: it only matters what these men in the first century thought."

"The one takes precedence over the other, yes." Cyril clarified.

"So, logically, we don't need to concern ourselves any longer with whatever God told Noah about blood (just as we don't need to concern ourselves over what he told him about having children.) It only matters what these men in the first century had to say about it. If they had said the blood law had passed away, then sister Foley would be alive today. Correct?"

"Well, yes, I guess so," Klaus hesitantly admitted.

"What's your point?" Henderson demanded, giving David a stern look.

"My point is that everything hinges on whether these men in the first century thought that "abstain from blood" meant only in the circumstance they found themselves in, or if they meant it to apply to everyone forever. That's all that matters since at least one law given to Noah is no longer in effect."

"They meant it to apply to all mankind forever," Cyril stated.

"How can we know that?" David wondered. "Maybe the key is in the other laws they laid down along with the blood law."

"Yeah," Bruce said, "they said to abstain from fornication. We know that's a law for everyone for all time, and so the law to abstain from blood must be too; one is just as important and binding on present-day Christians as the other."

"But what about this law to abstain from meats offered to idols?" David asked.

"What about it?" Hershey asked with a yawn, feigning disinterest.

"Don't you think it's pretty important since it's the first part of the sentence dealing with blood?" David asked. "Doesn't the verse read: 'That ye abstain from meats offered to idols, and from blood...'?"

"It does say that," Klaus agreed.

"But wasn't this *abstaining from meat offered to idols* just a law designed for the sole purpose of preventing the Christians from offending the Jews?" David asked. "And didn't Paul later write that it was really okay to eat meat offered to idols as long as no one was around who might be offended by such an action?"

"Yes," Klaus replied, this time having to thumb through his old worn *King James Bible* to find the obscure passage. "Here it is in *First Corinthians*:

"'As concerning therefore the eating of those things that are offered in sacrifice unto idols, we know that an idol is nothing in the world, and that there is none other God but one. Howbeit there is not in every man that knowledge: for some with conscience of the idol unto this hour eat it as a thing offered unto an idol; and their conscience being weak is defiled. But meat commendeth us not to God: for neither, if we eat, are we the better; neither, if we eat not, are we the worse. But take heed lest by any means this liberty of yours become a stumblingblock to them that are weak.' (1Cor. 8:4,7-9)"

"Thank you," David said with a smile and a nod to Klaus. "Paul said he was at liberty to eat meat sacrificed to idols, but that Christians needed to be careful not to offend those who didn't understand this freedom. So, evidently the "law" against eating meat sacrificed to idols was not a law binding on all mankind for eternity: it was just a recommendation for the circumstances of that particular time (when first century Christians were living amongst Jews and Jewish converts who had been taught their whole lives to abstain from meat sacrificed to idols.)"

"Well, yes," Klaus agreed, "I think that's true."

"So, then," David concluded, "nothing prevents us from saying the very same thing about the next part of the sentence: "abstain from blood". It was simply a recommendation to keep from offending the Jews: not a law binding on all mankind for eternity."

The men thought about this for a while, struggling to come up with a defense for their stance on blood.

Finally, it was Cyril who spoke up: "David, you're looking at this all wrong: as if abstaining from blood were some kind of hardship on Christians. In reality, blood transfusions are deadly poison: they kill people, change their personalities, pass loathsome diseases such as AIDS –"

"But none of that is a theological argument," David replied.

"It's a matter of our loving father Jehovah taking care of us, his children," Henderson said. "He has warned us against blood for our own good. It is a sin that defiles our bodies as well."

"But just a moment," David interjected. "Didn't your Jesus say 'There is nothing from without a man, that entering into him can defile him: but the things which come out of him, those are they that defile the man.'?"

"Yes, in Mark 7:15," Klaus replied.

"Well," David said, "if '*nothing*' entering into a man can defile him, then blood entering into a man can't defile him.

"Sister Foley died. Her doctor told me that blood would've saved her life. He explained the reason to me, and I understood the truth of it. There was no sense in which her having a transfusion would've 'defiled' her. It would've been the gift of life. Surely Jehovah wants us to live, gentlemen?"

"There are times," Henderson replied, "when Jehovah expects his people to sacrifice their lives to prove their faith. Sister Foley was privileged and honored to have done so."

"But if God is all-knowing, why would he require such a test of one's faith?" David asked.

"I see what you mean, Bruce," Henderson said, "one question leads to another with this one, and you don't end up getting anywhere."

"Why *don't* we drop the prohibition on blood?" Klaus asked. "I never did see the need for it. It was that medical quack that Rutherford had: he started the whole thing; made that big stink about vaccinations too. Maybe it's time we dropped all of that. It was always obvious to me that pouring out the blood of an animal was done as a sign of respect for the *animal's* life: an acknowledgement that life belongs to Jehovah. It was never the idea that blood could somehow harm the recipient. It was never about *us*."

"What are you saying?" Hershey asked in shock. "Blood transfusion is against God's law: a disfellowshipping offense."

"Well, so were organ transplants at one time," Henderson said, "until we changed our minds.

"Actually, I've been thinking along the lines of dropping the blood prohibition for some time. The problem is the possible lawsuits. If we were to back-peddle on this issue now, we'd have a lot of upset people out to sue us for 'wrongful death' or some such nonsense.

"It would also damage our credibility, perhaps beyond repair. Think of the people who have lost loved ones on this issue. Now if we were tell them that we made a mistake and transfusions never were against God's law, and their loved ones died for nothing—"

"Yes," Cyril added, "think of those parents who stood by and watched their children bleed to death because of our teaching. Surely at least some of them would turn on us."

"Which is more important," David asked: "your money and credibility or people's lives? What happened to sister Foley was *your* fault, and if you are honorable men you will do all that you can to make sure no one else has to die for your mistake."

At that moment the sound of a distant explosion was heard. David, who had a clear view out the window from his position at the head of the table, stared in horror. Then he jumped to his feet, turned and ran out of the room without shutting the door behind him.

"What's going on *now*?" Henderson asked in exasperation as he turned to take in the sight behind him.

"Look at that!" Cyril cried, pointing a shaking finger out the window.

The men gathered at the window and peered out in amazement, their gaze focused across the water to Manhattan.

"Armageddon has truly begun," Klaus said. "Let us rejoice!"

## 14

It was three days before anyone at Bethel laid eyes on David again.

It was during the Governing Body's afternoon meeting: brother Reese had just laid flat out on the conference table a copy of the book *Paradise Restored!* opened to an illustration of Armageddon. The crude line drawing depicted a skyscraper on fire with people falling to their deaths.

"This is exactly what we saw," he said. "The picture itself was prophetic. Jehovah guided the hand of the artist to show us just what the start of Armageddon would look like from our window!"

"That's what we've been trying to tell you brothers for days!" Hershey said.

Their gaze at the book was suddenly interrupted when a disheveled David, clad in dirty overalls, burst into the room.

For a moment no one recognized him: his white robe having become synonymous with him.

"Oh, look!" Hershey said sarcastically at last, "it's his royal highness, King David!"

"Shall we bow?" Reese chimed in, with a snort.

"Where have you been?" Henderson demanded.

"And where did you get those awful clothes?" Hershey asked with a scornful laugh.

"You smell like soot!" Reese added, pinching his nose shut to drive home the point.

David brushed off his sleeve, creating a gray dust cloud, causing Reese to let go of his nose and cough in earnest.

"A more pertinent question," David said, "would be: where have *you* been?"

"More *im*pertinence from the fraud," Hershey said angrily.

"No one asks the Governing Body where it's been!" Reese added indignantly.

"But I'll ask *you* again," Henderson said, measuring out his words with evident effort to contain his anger. "Where have you been?"

"I've been at Ground Zero," David replied calmly. "I was surprised and disappointed that I did not see any of you there lending a hand."

"Lending a hand?" Cyril exclaimed.

"We don't assist those whom Jehovah is destroying," Bruce explained. "That would be working against the Divine Plan."

"That might be a disfellowshipping offence, come to think of it," brother Hershey noted, visibly brightening.

"Well, actually I was prevented from helping by a woman police officer," David explained. "When I got there the second tower had already been hit, and people were evacuating both buildings. There was a yellow ribbon marking off the area, and police were making sure that everyone stayed behind it."

"Well, that's good anyway," brother Klaus commented, "it seems Jehovah had a hand in keeping you from taking the false step of helping his enemies."

"Not entirely," David said.

"What do you mean?" Henderson asked.

"I asked the officer what I could do to help," David explained, "and she told me to donate blood."

"Donate blood?" Reese shouted in disbelief.

"Yes, she said that there's never enough blood, and that the need would be much greater than normal for the next few days as the victims of the tragedy poured into the local hospitals. So I found a nearby Red Cross station and gave blood."

"Well, you're disfellowshipped, then," Hershey told him.

"I see," David calmly replied.

"It didn't take you three days to donate blood," Henderson said. "What have you been doing all this time?"

"Well, I'm not answerable to you for my time," David replied, "Especially if I'm disfellowshipped."

"David," Bruce said gently, "would you tell me, please, as a friend, where you've been?"

"I went back to Ground Zero and did what I could: serving the firefighters with food and water, helping cart away some of the rubble, comforting the cadaver dogs: things like that. One of the workers also did me a kindness by giving me these clothes, since my tunic was ripped and bloody."

"We can't help Jehovah's enemies," Bruce said. "You of all people should know that. The Bible tells us to rejoice when God destroys the wicked—"

"The children in the daycare of the Twin Towers were *wicked*?" David asked in astonishment.

"Their parents chose to keep them from the Truth," Cyril replied. "Just as the wicked people in Noah's day were all destroyed for not being on the ark: children included. Today, our organization is the ark of salvation. Those not in this organization will die at Jehovah's hand as surely as those in Noah's day. That's why Jesus said our day was just like Noah's day."

"I've been reading that story," David said. "As I understand it, those people were destroyed not because they weren't on Noah's ark: they were destroyed for being *wicked*. The ark was just the means of delivering the righteous. The act of getting on the ark was not what *made* them righteous."

"That's just splitting hairs," Hershey said. "The point is: people in the ark were saved: those outside of the ark died."

"But those outside of the ark were wicked, were they not?" David asked.

"Yes."

"And they were wicked before Noah ever started building his ark?"

"Yes."

"Then the ark had nothing to do with deciding who would be destroyed: people were destroyed solely on the basis of whether they were wicked."

"Okay, so what's your point?" Reese demanded.

"If you insist that our day is the same as Noah's day, then only the wicked will be destroyed." David explained.

"That's right," Henderson agreed.

"So, were these children in the daycare wicked or not?" David asked.

"They must've been," Klaus concluded with conviction.

"What about the 2-year olds? Were they wicked?"

"Evidently," Klaus replied.

"And the infants?" David asked.

Even brother Klaus was too ashamed to answer this.

"From one man sin entered into the world, and death through sin," Hershey quoted, "so that all men die. That applies to all ages. We all deserve death; we're born in sin. It is only through Jehovah God's loving arrangement of sacrificing his son that we have a chance to live forever. If the children of the goats perish along the way, we are not to lose any sleep over the matter. Far from it; it just means there are less of these two-legged germs running around."

"And through our witnessing work we have separated the sheep from the goats: those who have accepted our invitation and have come inside the organization are the sheep: and those outside are the goats." Reese added.

David took a slow, sweeping glance around the room, briefly meeting all of the men's eyes. "So you're all going to sit there and tell me that trying to help these unfortunate victims, and donating blood, and refusing to 'rejoice' in the deaths of infants—all of that is *wrong*?"

"Listen to him, brothers!" Hershey shouted, "This is the man posing as King David! King *David*, who wiped out entire Philistine villages, leaving no survivors to tattle on him—all the while he was a guest of the Philistine king. But this imposter can't stomach the death of a few goats! Is this going to wake the rest of you up finally?"

"Brother Hershey," Henderson said angrily, "for better or for worse this is King David back from the dead. The *Watchman* is on record on this matter. We'll just have to keep him from expressing his views in public: he'll just serve as a figurehead."

"But he gave blood!" Hershey reminded them in pleading tones.

"Oh, you can't disfellowship King David," Klaus noted with a chuckle.

"Besides: giving blood isn't the same as having a transfusion," Bruce noted.

"But it's not pouring it out onto the ground either," Reese commented.

"That's a Mosaic Law, and we all know that passed away." Bruce said.

"Then you're claiming that it's okay to store blood?" Reese asked.

"Why not?" Bruce asked.

"The *Watchman* is on record as having stated that the brothers must not store their own blood for possible use in future transfusions because storing blood is against the commandment to pour blood onto the ground."

"Well, that's part of the Mosaic Law, and the *Watchman* is also on record as having stated that the Mosaic Law passed away and is not applicable to Christians." Bruce countered.

"Well, it seems to me, in any case," David added, "that the *Watchman's* record for being right in the past is very poor. So, if it contradicts itself on this matter, and following it would lead to not lifting a finger to help those in need, then I say it should be ignored."

"Ignore the *Watchman*?" Cyril asked in astonishment.

"Yes," David replied with a smile, "why don't you decide for yourselves what is right?"

"Luke 12:57," Klaus gave the citation automatically without thinking. Then he thought about it and his mouth dropped open: "Jesus said that!" he remarked.

## 15

Later that day Jonathan Ingles was called to Bruce Kline's office.

"The Governing Body has another special assignment for you," Bruce told him. "We want you to serve as David's personal assistant."

"What does that mean, exactly?" Jonathan asked anxiously.

"Your days serving in the factory are over," Bruce explained. "You are to accompany David everywhere and never let him out of your sight."

"Okay."

"One other thing—"

"Yes?"

"He'll be mostly confined to his room, with a guard posted. For his own safety, of course."

"I see," Jonathan said, imagining terrorists trying to abduct the man from his room.

"And on those occasions when he does leave his room, we'd like him to have no contact with anyone but the members of the Governing Body."

"What do you mean 'no contact'?" Jonathan asked.

"We don't want him talking to anyone." Bruce replied, matter-of-factly.

"Oh, okay," Jonathan said hesitantly. "But what about his message for us?"

"That will be communicated in the usual way: through the Watchman publications."

Bruce's phone rang, and he gave Jonathan a dismissive gesture. "That's all for now. We've moved out your other roommates, and moved David into your room. He'll be less conspicuous there." Bruce picked up the phone and said, "Please hold." Then he covered the mouthpiece with his hand and gave Jonathan one last instruction: "report to me daily in my room after he's gone to sleep."

Jonathan nodded and left.

"Yes?" Bruce asked the caller, "this is brother Kline."

"This is Peter Frawley. I'm coming to do another interview with David today, and I'd like to stop in and talk to one of the Governing Body members as well."

"Oh, Frawley. We're all rather upset with you for what you wrote, and for not running it past us first."

"That's not the way a free press works, brother Kline." Peter replied.

"Maybe not, but that's the way Jehovah's organization works."

"Well, some of us have to work for a living, and that means operating in the real world. You don't get this kind of publicity without coming off a little odd. People want to read about the unusual and the controversial, and they're fascinated by conflict. Rutherford knew this, and went out of his way to court such stories.

"If the public perceives David as just another suit-and-tie briefcase-toting Watchman, you won't have a story. He can't be just your average Watchman who just happens to have been King David in his previous life. That's not news; people will only yawn at that: they'll dismiss it. He has to shake things up a bit. Especially now since 9/11 threatens to push all other stories into insignificance."

"Our PR department knows all of this quite well, thank you," Bruce replied. "But our needs for him have changed. We no longer consider him up for public consumption. He will act as an inspirational figurehead for Jehovah's name people. We don't care what the world thinks; Jehovah is destroying the world. The resurrection has begun and so has Armageddon. Or don't you read the papers?"

"I *write* the papers," Peter reminded him. "Can I talk to a Governing Body member today or not?"

"You're a little slow on the up-take, Frawley. You can't talk to a Governing Body member, and you can't talk to David anymore either."

"What about our deal?"

"This conversation is at an end." Bruce said, and hung up the phone.

## 16

Jonathan's room was standard issue: a small closet and a sink occupied the spaces immediately to the left and right of the door; two twin beds pushed against either wall took up the rest of the space.

The walls were bare of pictures. No television or phone, but next to a tiny mirror above the sink an ancient intercom hung on the wall. Ostensibly this was for announcements, but it was widely believed that the intercom could be switched on at anytime from the central office in order to monitor the brothers for "clean speech".

A clanging steam radiator and two large, venetian-blinded windows took up the wall opposite the door.

An additional bed could be rolled out from underneath Jonathan's bed to allow a third Bethelite to sleep. On those occasions the room would be wall-to-wall beds with no room to walk between them. Jonathan was glad at least that he now only had to share with *one* roommate, albeit a strange one.

David had quickly settled into Jonathan's room; his only possessions were his two changes of clothes and the toothbrush and razor Bruce had given him.

Having exhausted all of the small talk they could think of, they sat on their beds, staring dumbly out the window at the Hotel Margaret across the street.

"Would you care to go for a walk?" David asked.

"No, thanks," Jonathan replied quickly. He hoped it wouldn't be obvious too soon that he was acting as David's jailor.

"I made some friends across the street there that I'd like to talk with."

"What: at the Hotel Margaret?" Jonathan asked in surprise.

"Yes, I had a nice chat there the day after I arrived."

"Oh, we don't go there," Jonathan said; "it's a gay hangout."

"Well, no one's asking you to have sex with them; I'm just proposing conversation. I enjoy a good dialogue."

"Well, we can't go over there. You'll just have to talk to *me*. 'Bad associations spoil useful habits.'"

"Who says we can't go over there?" David asked.

"The Governing Body, that's who."

"But why do you let them decide for you what is right and wrong?"

"Because that's what a Governing Body does: it *governs*."

"But why have you chosen to let them govern *you*? Aren't you a free man?"

"Of course I'm free... and I've freely chosen to let them govern me."

"I see," David said thoughtfully. "But why have you freely chosen to give up your freedom?"

"Because they're the Faithful and Discreet Slave, that's why."

"And who is it that says they are such?"

"They do."

"That's what is known as *circular reasoning*, my friend."

"I don't want to talk about it anymore," Jonathan said, turning his head away.

David sighed, stood up, and said, "Well, I haven't chosen to give up *my* freedom, so I think I'll take a walk across the street."

"But I'd like you to stay here and talk to *me*," Jonathan pleaded.

"Didn't you just say you didn't want to talk?"

"Not about the Faithful and Discreet Slave class. But we could talk about something else. Why don't you tell me about killing Goliath?"

"As I explained to your 'slave' friends, I didn't kill Goliath."

Jonathan looked at him in astonishment. "You didn't kill Goliath? That's the one thing most people remember about you. That, and the fact that you wrote so many of the Psalms... and you told me before that you didn't write anything!"

"That's right," David replied. "Don't people ever make up things about *you*?"

"Yes, but the Bible writers didn't make anything up; they were inspired by Jehovah to write the truth."

"How do you know that?"

Seeing that Jonathan wasn't going to answer, David tried a different approach: "Here I am telling you that my killing Goliath is an untrue story. So, am I a liar then?"

"I don't know."

"Well, what do you *think*?"

"I think maybe the Faithful and Discreet Slave made a mistake in believing that you're King David back from the dead."

"Well, if they make mistakes, how can you surrender your freedom of choice to them? If they're wrong about me, what else might they be wrong about?"

"They never claimed to be perfect: everyone makes mistakes."

"Yes, but for a free man, at least his mistakes are his own."

"But I don't want God judging me for *my* mistakes," Jonathan explained. "If his organization makes mistakes, then he'll have to judge them accordingly, but he'll judge *me* on whether I was faithful to his organization or not."

"So, whether they're right or wrong, you feel that God wants you to follow them and their rules?"

"That's right."

"And you'll let them do your thinking for you: deciding what's right and wrong?"

"Yes," Jonathan replied with conviction. "We know that Jehovah judged the leaders of this organization to be the Faithful and Discreet Slave back in 1919. Now it's up to his Watchmen to remain true to his organization."

"How did you find out that Jehovah judged them in 1919? You weren't born yet, were you?"

"No."

"So, someone told you this?"

"That's right."

"Who?"

"The Faithful and Discreet Slave."

David sighed again. "That's more circular reasoning: it has no foundation but itself. Have you ever tried to pull yourself up by your bootstraps? It can't be done."

A long silence followed.

At last David said: "What if this 'slave' of yours gave you an order to kill me. Would you act on it?"

"They would never order us to do something immoral."

"How do you know?"

"I know."

"Yes, but *how*? If you've surrendered your freedom of choice to them, how can you determine that something is immoral? According to your stance, whatever this slave does would always have to be right, no matter what. If they told you to kill me, that would *have* to be the right thing to do."

"No, that would be wrong," Jonathan insisted.

"In order for you to say that," David explained, "you must be capable of determining what is right and wrong for yourself: independent of what the slave tells you."

"Yes, of course; all men know right from wrong. It is our God-given conscience that the Bible talks about."

"So then, you were mistaken earlier when you said that you let them determine right and wrong for you. In reality you follow them as long as they conform to your own notion of what is right."

"That's correct."

"So, in the end, you are the one determining what is right and what is wrong, and this whole business about relying on the 'slave' is a façade. You're not subject to them or reliant on their judgment; their authority over you is completely determined by *your* judgment of *them*."

Jonathan looked at David in surprise.

"They're not the ones in charge; *you* are," David concluded.

## 17

Bruce yawned and looked at his watch again. It was past his bedtime, and Jonathan still had not reported to him. He decided to take a stroll down to 5<sup>th</sup> floor and check on them.

He found the two large brothers he had appointed as guards dutifully standing on either side of Jonathan's door with vacant looks on their sleepy faces.

"Any trouble?" He asked them quietly.

They snapped to attention and the closest one reported, "They gave us a bit of trouble earlier."

"Wanted to go for a walk," the other added.

"We told them they'd have to stay put," the first brother proudly reported.

"The big one tried to push past us, but we shoved him back in the room and slammed the door."

"Haven't heard a peep out of them since then, but it might be a good idea to get a lock on the door from this side."

Bruce nodded and stepped close to the door, listening intently. He smiled as he heard the reassuring sound of snoring.

"Well, good night, brothers," he said, turning to go, "keep up the good work."

When he had gone the brothers looked at each other in dismay. "I thought he'd bring replacements. Does he expect us to stand out here all night with no sleep?"

The other frowned in response and said, "Remember when the apostles couldn't stay awake and watch with Jesus in the garden of Gethsemane? We don't want to be like that. Remember, brother: we're here in Jehovah's service."

"You're right. We'll stay here at our post until we're relieved... but maybe we can take turns sleeping."

"Okay, you take the first shift: wake me up in a couple of hours, or if you need me." And he lay down on the floor tight up against the wall.

Soon snoring could be heard on both sides of the door.

## 18

The following morning, at the Governing Body meeting, Bruce was relating his progress in negotiating the purchase of Beth-Sarim. "I'm afraid they are now asking for not a penny less than twelve-million in cash," he said.

"They must've discovered why we want it so badly," Klaus guessed.

"It's only money, brothers," Stingler said, "money will be worthless very soon in the New Order. I make a motion that we pay the twelve-million and not waste anymore time; Abraham and the rest could be resurrected any day now, and we really should have a welcoming house for them when they arrive."

"And how do you propose we pay for it?" Hershey asked.

"We can sell some land-holdings, or stock, I guess," Stingler replied.

"We've got over five-million shares in Rand Cam," Cyril stated. "Why don't we sell half of them: that would make up the difference, wouldn't it?"

"No," Henderson said, "it's only worth two million right now. But within a very few months they're almost certainly going to win that Navy contract to build more SWARM airplanes—"

"Especially after this 9/11 thing, with Bush clamoring for war," Hershey said.

"Yes," Reese added, "and don't forget the twenty-billion dollar potential of Rand's Machine Vision Technology; the department of defense is very interested in that for their "Intelligent Transportation System" missile-guidance. Right now we own fifty-percent of the company, so that's a potential ten-billion dollars if we hang on to the stock."

"Can you imagine any of the rank and file hearing this conversation?" Klaus mused, shaking his head.

"That's why they're not privy to such information," Henderson explained. "They'd have a hard time understanding how we use what Jehovah provides without questioning it: if stock is given to the Society which happens to be connected to the military, well that's just Jehovah letting us profit from the old world's destruction."

"Just like how we're secretly associate members of the United Nations," Klaus said. "You'd be surprised how many brothers are stumbled by that, after we've identified the U.N. as the image of the Wild Beast of Revelation."

"We're getting sidetracked here," Henderson said. "We can work out the details of how we come up with the money later. Right now I would like a vote on Stingler's motion to buy back Beth-Sarim for twelve million."

"I second the motion," Klaus said.

"All in favor?" Henderson asked.

All hands went up except for Hershey and Reese.

"Carried," Henderson decreed.

Just then Cyril burst into the conference room brandishing the *New York Times*.

"Has anyone seen this?" he demanded.

"What now?" Henderson asked with annoyance.

"Look!" Cyril cried as he held out the paper with the headline:

| **"King David" Held Prisoner at *Watchman* HQ** |
| --- |

"How did that leak out?" Bruce cried.

"It's by that Frawley fellow," Cyril explained, with a look of accusation directed at Bruce.

"Don't look at me," Bruce said, "I gave him the boot the other day."

"Excuse me, brothers," said Lois as she poked her head in at the door.

"Yes? What is it?" Henderson barked.

"The police are here in the lobby," Lois replied gently, "and they want to speak to 'whoever's in charge.'"

Henderson heaved a heavy sigh, and looked slowly around the room with a scowl. "Bruce, come with me," he ordered.

Henderson stood up and walked quickly out of the room, with Bruce making haste to follow. Then they stood in awkward silence waiting for the elevator to take them down to the lobby. When it arrived Henderson stepped briskly in and said, "You'd better come up with something good to get us out of this."

"We'll let Jehovah instruct us what to say," Bruce replied smugly, causing Henderson to scoff.

The elevator stopped once on third floor, but Henderson motioned the surprised Bethelites to wait, "Take the next one," he said, as he repeatedly pressed the *close-door* button.

The moment the elevator door opened on first floor they saw a large, muscular, uniformed officer and a man in a sports coat standing in the lobby waiting for them.

"Hello," Henderson said in a cheery tone, firmly shaking the hand of the sport-coated man. "I understand you gentlemen are asking who's in charge here."

"Yes, would that be you, sir?"

"No. Jehovah God is in charge here," Henderson replied, smiling even more broadly. "We're just carrying out his work to the best of our abilities."

"I see. Well, I'm Detective Kramer, and this here is Officer O'Rielly of the NYPD."

"Pleased to meet you both," Henderson replied, though of course he wasn't, and he didn't so much as glance at Officer O'Rielly. "And what can we do for you gentlemen?"

"And your name, sir?" Detective Kramer asked, making it clear who would be asking the questions.

"I am Henry Henderson." It was the first time in years that Bruce had heard him utter his first name.

"And you, sir?" He said without looking up from his notebook where he was busily writing.

"Bruce Kline, at your service."

Hearing the name, he looked up suddenly and studied Bruce's face for a moment. Then he resumed his routine manner, saying: "Fine. Now, can either of you gentlemen tell me anything about the whereabouts of one David Jesseson?"

Bruce couldn't help but react to the name with a laugh.

"Something funny, sir?"

"Yes. Wherever did you get that name?"

"From the complainant. He names you too, Mr. Kline, as the principal instigator of the kidnapping."

"Kidnapping!" Henderson and Bruce both exclaimed.

"Do you know the whereabouts of this man, or not?" Detective Kramer asked, looking first at one man and then the other.

"We have no such man here." Henderson said with conviction.

"How many men do you house here, sir?"

"Oh, it's well over a thousand."

"And you know instantly, without checking, that this particular name is not on your register somewhere?"

"Oh, we're just one big happy family here," Bruce replied.

Just then a crowd of brothers were walking past them on their way to the factory. Detective Kramer gave a nod to officer O'Rielly who put a hand up and stopped one of the passers-by. "Excuse me, sir," he said, "Detective Kramer would like to detain you for a moment."

"Am I in some sort of trouble?" the brother asked, visibly shaken.

"Not at all, young man," Detective Kramer assured him. "Just stand there a moment and let these two men take a good look at you."

"What's the point of this?" Henderson asked, his smile fading.

"Could either of you kindly tell me this young gentleman's name?" Detective Kramer asked, his pencil poised to write it down in his notebook.

Bruce and Henderson looked at each other and saw that neither of them had a clue.

Detective Kramer waited an embarrassing moment, and then said, "Alright, son, you can go." Then he turned to Henderson again and said, "One big, happy family, huh?"

"You're welcome to examine our role of residents," Henderson replied. "But I know you'll find no such person on it."

"I'll take your word on that," Detective Kramer said in a dismissive tone. "You're the publishers of the *Watchman* magazine, are you not?"

"We are," Henderson admitted.

"O'Rielly," Detective Kramer said, turning to the officer, "could you read from the article please?"

Officer O'Rielly took a rolled-up *Watchman* out of his back pocket, and read:

---

**King David Resurrected! Armageddon has Begun!**

---

Jehovah's name people long ago prophesied the resurrection of the "Ancient Worthies": those men of faith who talked with God in times of old. So certain were the Watchmen of the return of these Worthies that officials of the Watchman Society purchased a beautiful mansion in San Diego, putting the deed in King David's name. They respectfully dubbed it *Beth-Sarim*: The House of Princes.

Today the *Watchman* is pleased to announce the fulfillment of this prophecy in September of this year! During a convention of Jehovah's people, King David appeared at Beth-Sarim, dressed in a beautiful white robe! A member of the Governing Body was divinely directed to greet him upon his arrival and accompany him to the convention where King David addressed thousands of Jehovah's Watchmen and people of goodwill with the message that Jehovah's Day of Vengeance—*Armageddon*—has arrived!

Following the convention, King David was brought to Bethel, the world headquarters of Jehovah's Watchmen, in New York—

"Yes," Henderson interrupted, "you don't have to read the entire article; we wrote it, and know what it says perfectly well."

"But in that article," Detective Kramer pointed out, "it says that this David came here—for I am given to understand that this is the place you call Bethel, is it not?"

"Yes, yes, this is Bethel: the House of God," Henderson said proudly.

"Well, then, this David was here at some point," Detective Kramer concluded. "The question is: is he here *now*, and if so, is he being held against his will."

"Excuse us, Detective Kramer," Bruce replied, "but this isn't at all the question you asked at first. You were asking about a David Jesseson—"

"That's the surname I wrote in the complaint," said Peter Frawley, who had walked in the front door, unnoticed.

"I asked you to wait in the car, sir," Detective Kramer told him with evident annoyance.

"I thought you could maybe use my help," Peter replied, and then addressing Bruce, said: "I knew that you'd know who was meant since David is Jesse's son. You see," he said, addressing Detective Kramer again, "surnames were not used in the Bible. All they would say is so-and-so son of so-and-so."

"Look," Detective Kramer said impatiently, "we're not here to debate your religious beliefs, or have a Bible lesson. We're here to investigate a complaint: to determine if a felony has been committed, and ascertain if this man, whatever his name is, is being held against his will."

Bruce scowled at Peter, and then addressed Detective Kramer: "We have a man staying with us—of his own free will—whose name is David, and he is Jesse's son. Is that whom you'd like to see?"

"I would like to speak to this man alone," Detective Kramer said matter-of-factly. "I just need you to take me to him."

Bruce looked to Henderson for guidance. Henderson shrugged and said, "Very well," but *this* man," pointing to Peter, "must wait here."

Detective Kramer nodded his assent, and Henderson led the way back to the elevator.

As Bruce walked past Peter he whispered, "Consider yourself disfellowshipped for this stunt."

The two policemen and the two religious men rode silently up to the fifth floor, and then down the hallway towards Jonathan's room.

The two brothers standing guard looked surprised when they saw officer O'Rielly, and decided they'd better keep quiet.

"This is the room, here," Bruce told them, as he stepped up to the door and knocked.

"What are you two men doing here?" Detective Kramer asked the guards.

"They were making sure no one would disturb David," Bruce explained. "Lots of curiosity-seekers and autograph-hounds out there, you know. You two can go back to work now."

"I'll take your names first," Detective Kramer told them, and when they gave them, he wrote them in his notebook.

Bruce knocked on the door again, waited a moment and then tried the knob. The door was unlocked, so he pushed it open and called, "Hello!"

Detective Kramer followed close on his heels, and then Henderson and Officer O'Rielly.

The four men found themselves in an otherwise empty room.

"Call those two brothers back, Kline!" Henderson ordered.

For a moment Bruce thought he meant that he should call back David and Jonathan. He wondered how he was expected to do that—then he realized he meant the two brothers who had stood guard.

Bruce ran out the door and down the hall calling "Brothers, wait!"

They turned in unison and stared at him blankly. They didn't know what strange request to expect from him next.

When he caught up to them he took a moment to catch his breath, and the brothers had time to see the momentarily undisguised panic in his face.

"When did they leave the room? Where did they go?"

"No one left," they both replied.

"Of course they left; they're gone," Bruce yelled. "Did you leave your post?"

"No, sir," they both replied.

"And neither of you saw them leave?" Bruce asked, his eyes widening.

"They didn't get past us." The taller of the two said confidently.

"Kline! Get down here!" Henderson called from down the hall.

Bruce ran back towards Jonathan's room where the other men were waiting for him.

As Bruce caught his breath, Henderson looked at him sternly and said, "The law wants to know where you've put David."

"In this room, under guard," Bruce replied, growing pale.

"Did those two see him leave?" Henderson asked.

"No."

"The windows are locked from the inside, sir," Officer O'Rielly told Detective Kramer.

Detective Kramer looked at the men expectantly.

Henderson looked at Bruce for an answer, but when he saw only confusion he said, "Jehovah took them."

Detective Kramer wrote this down. "Now, who is this Jehovah, and where can we find him?" he asked.

Bruce was too shocked at what Henderson was suggesting to notice the absurdity of the detective's question. "Why would Jehovah 'take' them?" he asked.

Henderson took a deep breath and offered the following explanation: "We know that in the Millennium, which follows Armageddon, Jehovah God will judge people, and will destroy those who are disobedient to the leadings of his spirit. Doubtless he will do this in such a way that all trace of them will be gone, and there'll be nothing left of them for his obedient people to remember them by—or to bury."

"But, King *David*?" Bruce asked in disbelief.

"You yourself know that David had a rebellious nature. He was questioning the policies of God's earthy organization. Such a nature may have served him well in battles against the Philistines, but was inappropriate to his place in the organization in this phase of Jehovah's Divine Plan. We tried to reason with him to no avail. He had his chance, and Jehovah has judged him unworthy of everlasting life. So, he's gone."

"And Jonathan Ingles?" Bruce asked.

"Led into apostasy due to his close association with David. Jehovah destroyed them both."

All three men stared at Henderson in disbelief.

"Well, has anyone got a better explanation?" Henderson asked.

"Guards leave their posts, they fall asleep on duty, sometimes they even accept bribes," Detective Kramer offered.

"They wouldn't dare!" Henderson exclaimed.

"I'm afraid the law doesn't recognize supernatural events, gentlemen," Detective Kramer said, "I need you to produce David Jesseson right here and right now, or I'm afraid I'll have to take you both into custody."

"On what charge?" Henderson demanded indignantly.

"Obstruction of justice, suspected kidnapping, and hopefully nothing more sinister."

He nodded to Officer O'Rielly who produced two pairs of handcuffs and instructed Bruce and Henderson to turn around and give him their hands.

"Don't worry, brother Kline," Henderson said as the cuffs snapped into place "the Society's lawyers will have us out in no time."

**19**
*(September 16, 2001)*

The following day an emergency meeting of the Governing Body was called to address the issue of the brothers' imprisonment.

Cyril, as next in line for the role of chairman, took Henderson's position at the head of the table. "I've alerted our lawyers to the situation," he said, "so now our main order of business is how to announce David's destruction."

"Destruction?" they all exclaimed.

"Yes, brother Henderson had a long discussion with me on the phone from the precinct. He and brother Kline determined that destruction by Jehovah for apostasy is the only explanation for David's disappearance from his guarded room."

"Well, that will be another vindication of us," Stingler said. "We always taught that anyone who disobeyed Jehovah's will during the Millennium would be destroyed outright."

"This proves that no one is immune from Jehovah's justice," Hershey added.

"Or from apostasy," Klaus added with a tinge of sadness.

"That should put the fear of God back into the brothers," Reese concluded.

"It also vindicates us on the blood issue," Hershey noted with a smile.

"Maybe we should consider revising our interpretation of the two witnesses in prison," Reese suggested. "No member of the Governing Body has been in prison since Rutherford, and he had to fudge the dates to fit *his* interpretation. This is potentially a much better fulfillment of Scripture."

"That has potential," Cyril agreed.

"I make a motion that we get the writing committee on this right away," Cyril said.

"I second it," Stingler said.

"All in favor?" Cyril asked, and all hands went up.

Just then Lois wrapped on the door and poked her head in. "Excuse me, brothers, there's a young Bethelite out here to see you. He says it's urgent."

"Sister Lois," Reese said sternly, believing he was speaking for them all. "We just can't tolerate these continual interruptions. We have important matters to decide here. Bethelites can see one of the committees appointed to deal with their petty problems."

"Okay," Lois said, the tears welling up in her eyes. "Brother Henderson never spoke to me in that tone. But I'll just tell young brother Ingles that you don't have time to see him." And she disappeared out the door.

"Ingles... Ingles," Klaus said slowly. "Wasn't that the name of the boy that brother Kline put in charge of David?"

"Yes," Cyril said, "Jonathan Ingles. Brother Henderson told me that he went missing the same time as David. They figured Jehovah had destroyed both of them for apostasy. I was going to call his family today and let them know."

"Good thing you waited," Hershey chuckled.

"Well, if he's not destroyed," Stingler said, stating the obvious, "maybe David isn't either."

"We'd better wait on any announcement then," Klaus said, "until we get to the bottom of what exactly is going on."

"Yes, I think we'd better," Cyril agreed, trying not to sound sarcastic. "Brother Reese, would you be so kind as to ask Lois to send him in."

Reese, flushed with anger, stormed out the door. Titters of suppressed laugher followed.

"A little crow before dinner, brother Reese?" Klaus asked, and the other men laughed heartily—except for Hershey who stared at him with a contemptuous look.

When Reese returned with Jonathan they sat him at the far end of the table and Cyril began interrogating him.

"Where is David?"

"At the police station, last I saw him."

"And how did he come to be there?"

"He wanted to go for a walk, and resented not being allowed to. I resented it too. So we waited till our guards were both asleep, and we left."

"Where did you go?"

"Oh, David had made some friends across the street at the Hotel Margaret, so we went over there to talk with them. We talked late into the night, and then one of the men there was kind enough to take us in and allow us to sleep in his room overnight. In the morning we went to Central Park and talked to people there."

"Did you place anything?" Klaus asked.

"No, we just talked."

"*Witnessed*, you mean?" Stingler asked.

"No, not really. David just talked and listened. It wasn't like witnessing at all."

"What else did you do yesterday?" Cyril asked.

"And where did you spend the night?" Klaus asked. "This is a very dangerous, sinful city, young man."

"Well," Jonathan said, his voice faltering, "I don't think I'm going to tell you anymore about it."

"Why not?"

"Because when it comes to *me*, *I'm* in charge: not *you*," Jonathan said, swallowing hard, "and I choose not to tell you."

"Isn't that rather headstrong?" Cyril asked trying to sound solicitous.

"And puffed up with pride, I'd say!" Klaus added in disgust.

"No," Jonathan replied, "I'm just making the point that I don't owe you an explanation. I don't have to report everything I do to you."

"Who taught you such insubordination? Was it David?" Reese asked.

"He got me to thinking, yes," Jonathan admitted.

"Now he's corrupting the youth," Hershey commented.

Anyway," Jonathan continued, "this morning we saw the newspaper article about how he was being held prisoner, and he insisted we go to the police station right away and clear the matter up."

"Did you know that your little walk cost brothers Henderson and Kline their freedom? Hershey shouted. "They were arrested on charges of kidnapping!"

"Well, excuse me, brothers," Jonathan replied, as meekly as he could manage, "but surely our walk wasn't the cause of that. We didn't ask to be imprisoned in my room. That wasn't *our* doing."

"Are you implying that the chairman of the Governing Body deserved to be incarcerated because you were slightly inconvenienced?" Reese demanded.

"If you'd stayed put," Klaus said, "as you were told to do, the policemen would've found you in the room where we expected you, and they wouldn't have hauled our dear brothers off in handcuffs imagining that they'd killed you both off or some such nonsense!"

"I'm sorry that happened," Jonathan said, "but you had no right to keep us locked up."

"You weren't locked up!" Hershey shouted. "Don't lie on top of everything else!"

"Well, we weren't locked up by *hardware*," Jonathan admitted, "unless you want to call those lugs outside our door hardware."

"Now you refer to your brothers as 'lugs'?" Stingler asked.

"They shoved me," Jonathan told them, "why don't you council *them* instead?"

"You just worry about yourself," Hershey told him. "You're in no position to judge anyone. Imagine Judas complaining about the other apostles!"

"I'm no Judas," Jonathan stated firmly.

"No?" Reese said, "Then why did you go to the police station to tattle on your brothers?"

"You were privileged to have been given a responsibility: a task was assigned to you by a member of the Governing Body. And what did you do, young man? Did you faithfully carry out your duty?"

"I didn't 'tattle'," Jonathan corrected, but before he could say more, Henderson, Bruce, and David stepped into the room.

"Praise Jah!" Klaus exclaimed upon seeing them.

"All charges have been dropped," Henderson explained, "and David has been released into our custody. Seems he wasn't destroyed after all."

"Nor was this one," Reese said, pointing to Jonathan. "But with the mouth on him, I can't imagine why Jehovah spared him."

Henderson walked slowly over to the window and gazed out at the vacant sky that used to be blocked from view by the World Trade Center.

"David and Jonathan, please go to your room," he said.

"With or without guards?" Jonathan made bold to ask.

"Without," Henderson replied, "but please, as a favor to us, please stay in your room until further notice."

David and Jonathan left quietly.

Henderson turned and faced them. "What are we to do, brothers?"

Hershey was the first to respond: "David has corrupted this youth."

"Yes, I can see that," Henderson acknowledged.

"And," Reese added, "he has introduced a new god: the god of reason in place of faith in Jehovah and his organization."

Klaus said: "He's teaching people to reject our God-given authority and 'do their own thing,' as was in painful evidence in the actions of his protégé over the last few days. Before you arrived, brother Henderson, this youngster was actually talking back to us!"

"I'm mostly worried about his challenging us on the blood issue," Cyril said. "That could have major repercussions."

"Still think we can afford to let him write his own material?" Henderson asked Bruce in a sarcastic tone.

**20**

*(October 7, 2001) (Three weeks later)*

Bruce stood behind a stage curtain with Henderson, Hershey, and Klaus, peeking out at the thousands of people filling the auditorium at the special winter assembly in New York. The assembly had been called because David's existence was attracting so many into the fold, and so many were thirsting to see and hear him.

The writing committee had come up with a speech for David to give, and Bruce had helped him practice it in his room in the evenings. David spent his days in the Bethel library with Jonathan, reading the Bible and devouring Watchman publications like a famished man consuming bread.

The speech itself sounded very much like last year's convention speech, except that there was a strong hint that Armageddon had already begun, and a brief mention of the fact that more Ancient Worthies were expected to be resurrected any day.

Bruce felt that David's oratory style was basically good, although he appeared slightly bored with the material.

Now the auditorium was packed with Watchmen and their "studies" who were longing to see King David with their own eyes, and hear his message. The media was also in full force, including Peter Frawley.

Brother Henderson was at the podium introducing David: "Brothers and sisters," he said, with a broad smile, "how privileged we all are to serve Jehovah at this time, here in God's spiritual paradise, soon to be a physical one as well!"

Only perfunctory applause greeted this statement. The crowd was anxious to see David.

"As you know, I have someone special I'd like to introduce to you today. Someone you've all read about in your studies of God's Word. Someone who *wrote* parts of God's Word! Someone who followed after the truth and served Jehovah all of his days. Someone who is here with us now as proof that the resurrection has begun!"

The audience took this as their cue and began applauding in earnest. But Henderson did not leave, and David did not appear. Realizing that Henderson had more to say, the applause stopped quicker than it had begun.

"Brothers and sisters," Henderson said, taking a long pause to increase the suspense, "I give you King David!"

Henderson stepped beside the podium, and turning to look offstage, joined the now riotous applause.

There was a long delay before he appeared. During that time the applause had time to die down somewhat, but when David finally walked onto the stage, the applause, shouting, and whistling renewed itself even louder than at first. Henderson walked towards him and met him halfway. Shaking his hand and clasping his shoulder, he ushered him over to the podium, then with one arm around David he turned to face the thousands of flashing cameras.

People were slightly disappointed to see him in modern attire, but the Governing Body had decided that a tunic was inappropriate for a New York winter, and of course they had destroyed his overalls as soon as the opportunity arose.

When the applause finally started to quiet down Henderson walked off the stage, leaving David standing alone behind the podium where his neatly typed-out speech and a Bible had been laid out for him.

Bruce was standing offstage as well, and turning to Henderson he said, "Let's hope the speech we've given him lives up to their expectations."

"I think he can do no wrong at this point," Henderson said, and the two men smiled at each other for the first time in a long time.

David stared out across the expanse of faces in all of their adulation. He looked warmed to his heart at feeling so needed. Then he briefly glanced at the first page of the speech, and strode away from the podium: walking upstage to be closer to the people who had come to see him.

"Brothers and sisters," David began, "your Bible says, 'Come, and let us reason together,' and today I want to do exactly that with you."

"What is he doing?" Henderson asked.

"It looks like he's adlibbing," Bruce said with a slight smile, though worry could be seen in his eyes.

"Yes, and ignoring our speech!" Henderson exclaimed.

"That's *Isaiah* 1:18 from the *King James Bible*," Klaus noted.

"He's not even quoting the *New World Translation*," Henderson complained.

"No," Hershey added, "our translation says: 'Come, and let us *set matters straight* between us,' that's quite a difference."

"The translation committee chose those words to eliminate the idea of human reasoning," Klaus stated.

"I'm going to put a quick stop to this!" Henderson said.

"If you do, I fear we'll have a riot on our hands," Bruce cautioned.

"I've got a solution here," Hershey said.

"What's your suggestion?" Henderson asked.

Hershey picked up the glass of water from a teacart that was waiting to be wheeled out to the podium. "A little something extra in here would cut his speech short."

"What you're suggesting is criminal," Bruce told him.

"We obey a higher law," Hershey responded, not taking his eyes off Henderson.

"Only if it comes to that," Henderson said softly. "And I'll be the one to decide if he goes too far."

The men focused their attention back on David, listening intently.

"Do we always do that?" David asked the crowd before him. "Do we always reason together? I think not. But let's try it for the next hour or so.

"According to your Bible it was said of me that I "slew my ten thousands". The first order of reasoning, by the way, is not to simply accept everything you hear, or believe everything you read, so I encourage you not to take such calumny at face value. I was a peaceful shepherd, given to music and poetry. Yes, I served my country in war when it needed me—something I'd be disfellowshiipped for today—but I was not a warrior.

"What they *really* said was: 'David *sang* his ten thousands' – of songs.

"Unlike me, my brothers were real soldiers, and as such they were trained to think of the enemy as something vile: something not human. Otherwise they would hesitate, and in battle that would've been fatal. A soldier must not think about the killing: he must not reason.

"But what different feelings are inspired by the face of a friend or kinsman! How could we ever consider killing a loved one? I say never could we consider such a thing unless we had been deprived of our reason. We have plenty of instances of madmen killing their families, but there are also instances in history where people, who otherwise appeared sane, killed a family member, or—what amounts to the same thing—allowed them to die when they might've lived healthy, meaningful lives.

"I contend that in every such instance reason had been abandoned or subverted.

"When my own son died, I would've done anything to prevent it.

"You'll recall from your Bible that my son supposedly died as a punishment for my sin with Bath-Sheba and Uriah. Of course this contradicts another passage in your Bible where it states that the son will not die for the sin of the father, so again I advise caution in your acceptance of this account.

"*Ezekiel* 18:19-20," Klaus whispered.

"We know," Henderson snarled.

"But, for whatever reason," David continued, "one of my sons was dying, and I would gladly have torn out my own heart and given it to him if that could've kept him alive.

"That was not possible then, but I understand that with your marvelous technology today transplants are now possible, and are permitted amongst you fine people. Isn't that right?" He turned to Henderson offstage to ask this question. Henderson stared back in confused anger, but Bruce nodded.

"I'm assured by members of the Governing Body offstage here that this is correct."

This was met with laughter and then by scattered applause. Usually it took months for an average Watchman to get any kind of answer to a question posed to the Governing Body. David made it appear so easy! But the real joke was how David was pretending that he needed to consult with them at all. The crowd was enjoying his informal delivery and how open he was being with them.

"Yes, people who are by nature loving—people such as yourselves—won't we do anything within our power to help? To give life and hold off death from our loved ones?"

"I want to tell you a little story," he said as he sat down at the edge of the stage. A couple of people rushed forward and touched the hem of his trousers, but they were shoved quickly away by the big brothers acting as security guards, and no one else dared make the attempt.

"The story," David continued, as if nothing had happened, "is about my introduction to your marvelous technology, namely the computer. A brother in the Bethel library took pity on my hopeless key-pressing, and showed me how to search the Internet. A truly wondrous thing!

"Knowing that I would be privileged to speak to you all today, I began doing research on this topic. Soon I came upon a website created by a man who lost his wife due to tragic circumstances: she died because he refused to allow her to have one of these transplants, although the doctors assured him that she would die without one.

"This man's reasoning had been subverted, my dear brothers and sisters. He had been misled into believing that transplants offended God and were 'cannibalism'.

"He listened to those who told him this as if they had some pipeline to God, and knew God's opinion on such matters. He was not 'reasoning together' with them; he was allowing them to do his thinking for him, and he was reduced to merely following their dictates. His reason had been surrendered. He was not following the Bible's admonition to 'reason together,' and the sad result is that he lost his wife.

"Now, of course, he regrets this. He wishes that he had used his reason back then, because now the men who told him transplants were a sin admit that they were mistaken! Now they say that transplants are *not* cannibalism, and are *not* against God's law!

"So, this man's wife died due to two mistakes in reasoning. The first was in the reasoning of these men who thought God was offended by transplants. The second mistake was made by the husband who surrendered his reason to these men, and failed to think for himself.

"The husband I'm speaking of was a Jehovah's Watchman, and the men I'm speaking of are the Governing Body of Jehovah's Watchmen."

Hoots and catcalls rang out from several areas of the crowd, causing Henderson to smile. These were the Bethel brothers he had planted in the audience to stir up resistance in case David criticized the Governing Body.

But no one joined in as Henderson had expected they would, and the security guards, whom Henderson had forgotten to clue in, soon quelled the noise.

"Why do you make such noises, when you know what I'm saying is true?" David asked in a calm tone. "I've been reading the *Watchman* in the Bethel library, and it very clearly prohibited transplants not that many bound-volumes ago, and these were the reasons that it gave. If any of you don't believe me, you can read the prohibition for yourself in the November 15th, 1967 *Watchman* on page 702. And then you can read the reversal of this stance in the March 15th, 1980 issue on page 31. Can anyone dispute this?"

He paused, but no one made a sound.

"Very well, then," he said.

"Don't criticize the Faithful and Discreet Slave!" One of Henderson's minions yelled out.

"Quiet!" others around him shouted.

"Let us continue to reason together, dear brothers and sisters," David said. "You see what happened to this man who didn't? I am not here to criticize anyone. The Governing Body is to be *commended* for correcting their misunderstanding in the matter of transplants. I salute them for this."

This brought a round of applause.

"No, brothers and sisters, I'm not here to criticize; I am here to reason with you, and point out the dire consequences when we fail to use our reason.

"What if you could go back in time a few years to when the Governing Body mistakenly held that transplants were a sin? What if you could contact this husband I've been telling you about? What would you tell him?"

An uncomfortable murmur passed through the crowd, but no one ventured to answer.

"Shall I tell you what I would do?" David asked, and was greeted with the applause of approval.

"I would tell this man the truth: that the Governing Body was mistaken, and that transplants were not against God's law, and that he should go ahead and let the doctors perform this life-saving operation on his wife. Isn't that what any ethical person would do?"

Another round of applause expressed the crowd's general approval.

"And what do you suppose would've happened to me then, in that scenario?" David asked.

"Disfellowshipped!" several called out.

"Yes, I fear you're right. I would've been disfellowshipped as an 'apostate' for stating the truth: a truth that contradicted the mistaken notion the Governing Body held at that time.

"That would've been sad for me: being shunned by you good people. But, I would've saved this woman's life. Wouldn't that have been more important than my status in your eyes?

"If I had been disfellowshipped by men, how would that affect my relationship with God? Would God prefer that I remain silent and allow this woman—this *sister* of mine—to die when I knew a truth that would save her life?

"Life is precious to Jehovah. That is why he said to pour out the blood of an animal: as a sign of respect for the life that was taken."

"We must be willing to sacrifice our lives for Jehovah!" Another stooge called out.

"In another verse of your Bible," David calmly replied, "I believe it's *Hosea* chapter 6, verse 6 (for those who want to check up on me), your God is represented as saying: 'I desired mercy, and *not* sacrifice.'

David waited, but was met with silence since none of the hecklers could think of any reply to this.

"My dear brothers and sisters," David continued, "a God of love does not want us to stand by and watch our loved ones die when we have the means to save them. And thank God—I mean the Governing Body—that we are all allowed to have transplants today!"

This brought on a long round of applause, though several people caught the deliberate slip-of-the-tongue and started to laugh as they clapped.

"Now, I want to remind you of something from the Watchman booklet entitled *How Can Blood Save Your Life*. On page 8 it states that a blood transfusion is a transplant."

Another murmur went up amongst the crowd.

"Why don't you talk about something you know about?" Another heckler got up the nerve to shout.

"Well, I know how to read," David said, chuckling. "If you doubt that, you're welcome to read the booklet for yourself, I assure you that you'll find that I'm not misrepresenting it. It clearly states that a transfusion is a transplant.

"Now, those of you who are reasoning with me have already reached an important conclusion. Who can tell me what it is?"

Hands went up all over the auditorium. David pointed to a young girl in the third row and said, "Yes, you please, sweetheart?"

She looked around to see if a roving microphone would be brought to her, and Henderson watched in surprise as one was. "What? Is this turning into some parody of a *Watchman* study meeting?" he asked.

Bruce just shook his head in dismay. He couldn't believe what he was seeing, and he wondered why Henderson hadn't taken steps to stop it before it had gotten to this point.

"If transplants are permitted," her young voice boomed out, causing a momentary shriek of feedback. She waited a moment for them to turn down the volume, as she had learned to do in her local Watchmen Hall, then started again, "If transplants are permitted, and transfusions are transplants, then transfusions are permitted."

"Yes, thank you," David said. "Now we are truly reasoning together.

"Recently I witnessed firsthand a tragedy very similar to the one I just told you about. I saw a man watch his wife die. Help was available for this woman: help that would've saved her life. Her life, I should add, was without chronic pain. It was a life surrounded by love, friends, and meaningful purpose. Yet the husband did nothing. More than that, he refused to allow others to help her to live.

"This man was another Jehovah's Watchman, and his wife died refusing a blood transfusion.

"Was this man reasoning? No, his reason had been subverted. I would say that one of the clearest indicators of subverted reasoning would be a person shunning a family member or allowing a family member to die in such circumstances. It proves without a doubt that such a person is not reasoning, but has allowed someone else to think for him.

"Knowing what we now know, thanks to our reasoning together, what if we could once again take a journey back through time—to that hospital room, and speak to that man. What would we say to him?"

Once again hands went up all over the auditorium, and David selected an elderly man in the middle of the auditorium to respond.

"King David," he began, "I've been an elder for thirty-five years, and based on what you've said today, I would tell this man that a blood transfusion was *not* against God's law."

The attendant began taking the microphone away when the elderly man grabbed it back and said, "And if they want to disfellowship me for that, they damn well can!"

People began clapping with their hands raised over their heads. Then they began standing: a few here and there at first, then suddenly the man was receiving a standing ovation from the vast majority of the audience.

"We're being made out to be the enemy," Hershey said. "Isn't it time we offered David a drink?"

Henderson starred at him a long time, and finally said, "Think of what you're suggesting!"

"This is theocratic warfare," Hershey replied.

"I'm not ready to go that far," Henderson said, trembling. "But by all means, let's pull the curtain on this!"

"Why don't we cut off his microphone," Klaus suggested. Then one of us can go out there and read *Acts* 15:20 without comment.

"An excellent idea!" Henderson exclaimed. "Kline: go tell the Ministerial Servant in charge of the audio to cut David's mike, and turn mine back on."

Bruce ran off to look for the brother as Henderson stepped back onto the stage.

David was in mid-sentence when his microphone went dead. Henderson was standing at the podium by that time, and immediately began rattling off the verse in question.

All had gone as planned, but the crowd seemed confused by the sudden change.

Henderson looked up with a smile of victory, but couldn't read the audience's reaction.

There was a tense moment of silence, and then Peter Frawley, who had been sitting in the front row, taking notes, raised his hand, and a well-trained brother brought the roving mike immediately to him.

Instead of speaking into the microphone, Peter grabbed it and handed it to David, still seated on the edge of the stage.

With mike in hand, David stood up and walked over to Henderson.

"Thank you, brother Henderson," he said, "for that Scriptural quote; it's exactly what I was going to say next. But now that I have a working microphone again I shan't need you to fill in for me anymore."

Henderson was aghast. He had imagined that reading the Scripture would put an end to David's talk, and bring the crowd back to its senses. But here he was being credited with having helped David out with the talk, and was now being dismissed like some flunkey!

"How can you say that blood-transfusions are not against God's law in light of that Scripture?" Henderson demanded.

"Yes," David replied, "that was the very question I was going to ask next," then turning to the audience, "It seems brother Henderson is bound and determined to help me give my speech. Let's have a round of applause for him."

The audience duly and politely applauded.

"But now, really," David said, addressing himself to Henderson, "please give me a vote of confidence. Show these fine people that you trust me enough to give my own speech. After all, Jehovah entrusted me with the role of king over Israel. Don't you think I can handle giving a speech on my own?" Then turning to the audience once again: "What do you think?"

The applause was in earnest this time. After a moment Henderson held up his hands to quiet them down, but the applause continued. They wanted to hear David.

Henderson began shouting into his microphone, but this only increased the volume of the applause. At last he gave up and walked off the stage. Only then did the applause cease.

David cleared his throat, and almost immediately brother Hershey wheeled out a teacart with a pitcher of water and a drinking glass on it.

"Thank you," David said, and laying the microphone down on the teacart, poured himself a glassful of water, which he quickly drained.

Picking up the microphone again, he said, "I once told my men to break the law: a law that I had already broken myself. Your Bible relates the story. In spite of that, it states that throughout my life (with the exception of the Bath-Sheba incident) I only did what was *right* in the eyes of the Lord.

"Jesus later used my example to justify the breaking of the Sabbath law by his men.

"Can we safely conclude from this that the statement '*break God's law*' is an order for all times, places, and circumstances?

"Of course not; this would go against everything you stand for!

"So, how do we explain this? The answer is a critically important word: *context*.

"My men and I were hungry. The sacred shewbread was the only food available. It was unlawful for anyone but the priests to eat it, but should we have died rather than break God's law? The verdict from your Bible is clearly No.

"So, if we come upon this incident in your Bible where I am breaking God's law and telling my men to break it as well, don't falsely conclude that this means it is okay for you to break God's law whenever you feel like it. No, you must consider the context.

"Let's take another example. This sport coat that brother Kline was kind enough to give me," he said as he removed the coat and held it so as to read the label on the collar. "The label here says that it is 85% polyester and 15% wool. Now, I ask you: is this a sinful garment? Am I breaking God's law by wearing it?

"In your Bible book of *Deuteronomy* chapter 22, starting in verse eleven, you will read that:

"'Thou shalt not wear a garment of divers sorts, as of woollen and linen together. Thou shalt make thee fringes upon the four quarters of thy vesture, wherewith thou coverest thyself.'

"This was God's law, and this polyblend coat with no fringes clearly violates that law. I'm sure if you looked at your clothing labels, many of you would also find yourself in violation of this law of God's from the Bible.

"Does anyone have a match so that I may burn this sinful sport coat?"

This was met with nervous laughter. No one was quite sure what to expect next, and some fully expected him to actually light the garment on fire. Others began planning a new single-fabric wardrobe based on this new ruling.

"But wait," David said with a smile; "this law, they tell me, *passed away*. It has expired. My coat is safe!" He chuckled and began putting it back on, but then changed his mind. "It's too hot under these lights," he said, and laid the coat atop the podium.

"But you'd never come to the conclusion that this law passed away just by reading this particular book of the Bible; listen to what is written in chapter 28 of that same book:

"'If you will not take care to carry out all the words of this law that are written in this book so as to fear this glorious and fear-inspiring name, even Jehovah, your God, Jehovah also will certainly make your plagues and the plagues of your offspring especially severe, great and long-lasting plagues, and malignant and long-lasting sicknesses.'

"That sounds pretty serious to me," he said, loosening his tie. "Note that it says to take care to carry out *all* the words of the law: not just the popular ones or the ones that make sense to us. 'All' would include the laws on polyblends and fringes. Yet here we are, thousands of Jehovah's Watchmen, supposedly obedient to his word, dressed in polyblend garments without a fringe in sight.

"How can we explain this?"

"Context," most of the audience replied.

"Yes, context," David agreed. He found his mouth filling with saliva, and he wanted to spit, but knowing that would be rude, he swallowed, and then swallowed again before continuing.

"You can't just go into the Bible and pick a verse here and a verse there—as I have just done—and expect to find the truth. Such a procedure ignores the context and can cause you to take destructive actions unnecessarily (like burning my sport coat.)

"Now let's return to the Scripture that brother Henderson was kind enough to read for us. There was a prohibition against blood. Yes, certainly there was. But what was the *context*? Was it something meant for all people for all times places and circumstances? Or was it specific to the particular time place and circumstance of the people who wrote it?

"Well, who were these words for? They were addressed to Gentiles who were becoming Christians in the midst of a Jewish population. We know that the Jews would've been horrified to see a Christian eat meat from a strangled animal that had not been ritually bled, or eat meat that had been sacrificed to an idol. It was with these Jewish sensibilities in mind that the Christians decided to abstain from such meat, and of course from directly drinking blood itself.

"But did they intend this as a law to last for eternity or to extend at all beyond those limited circumstances of time and place? To answer that, please open your Bibles to *First Corinthians*, chapter eight."

As the audience began searching for the passage in their Bibles, David walked a little unsteadily to the podium. He was feeling nauseous and dizzy, and was glad to lean against the podium for support. He picked up the *New World Translation* and started flipping through the pages in search of the passage while most of his audience continued flipping through their own worn copies of the book.

"While you're looking that up," David said, pausing to swallow several times again, "I want to tell you about a recent visit I paid—together with our dear brother Jonathan—to a local synagogue. There we spoke with the head rabbi, and I asked him if he thought any Jews would be offended at a Christian having a blood transfusion. He looked at us and said, 'The only thing that offends us is when Christians refuse life-saving medical techniques and claim that such disrespect for the sanctity of life is based on the Torah.'"

David turned his head to cough again, but this time he vomited.

Straightening up and wiping his mouth with the back of his hand, he began to say, "Excuse me, brothers and—" and then he collapsed to the floor of the stage. He lay face up with his eyes shut. Motionless for a moment, then his legs began to twitch and his hands to tremble. A wet spot formed at his crotch, and then his entire body began convulsing violently.

The crowd gave a collective gasp and many stood up in confusion.

"He's having a grand mal seizure!" someone called out.

Henderson ran out onto the stage waving his arms, "Brothers and sisters!" He cried, "Do not be alarmed! We are witnessing Jehovah's judgment. This is proof that we're now in the Millennium where Jehovah will destroy apostates immediately."

"Someone call 9-1-1!" A sister shouted. But Peter Frawley and several others with cell-phones already had.

"We'll cooperate with the authorities and let them take David to the hospital, of course," Henderson assured them. "But we know they'll be powerless to undo Jehovah's destruction of an apostate. Please go home now, brothers and sisters," he said as the stage curtain closed and only his disembodied voice remained, "and contemplate Jehovah's power and the dawn of the 1,000 year reign of Christ, secure in your association with God's organization on Earth, guided by the Faithful and Discreet Slave Class."

Peter managed to fling himself up onto the stage before the security guards could grab him. He ducked under the curtain just in time to see Hershey making a beeline for the teacart. Peter moved fast and got there a split second sooner. He grabbed the glass, then turned and headed towards David.

"Hey, that's stealing!" Hershey called, but the volunteer paramedics—always in the wings at such an event—were already running into view, so he stopped himself short.

"He's been poisoned," Peter told the first paramedic as she stooped over and began examining David.

"His pupils are dilated," the examining paramedic told the others. "Loss of bladder control... jaws clamped tight... convulsions... excessive saliva."

"Sounds more like water hemlock than strychnine," the older, male paramedic said.

"I think it was in this glass," Peter said, holding the glass out. "It looks like there's a few drops left."

The paramedic held out his hand and told Peter to pour a drop onto his finger. Then he touched the fingertip to his tongue and said, "It's sweet to the taste; my diagnosis is water hemlock. Get him to the ambulance stat. I'll see if they want us to give him a mega-dose of sodium pentobarbital on the way."

They placed David on the stretcher and rushed him out of the auditorium; with Peter following, glass in hand.

21

The next morning Bruce received a phone call from Peter.

"David is dead," he said.

"We knew it would happen," Bruce replied, "Jehovah destroyed him for apostasy."

"Maybe you knew it would happen because you poisoned him," Peter suggested.

"That's a very serious accusation. You'd better have something to back it up, or you'll be sued for slander—and for libel if you print it."

"They found hemlock in the water glass."

"Well, Jehovah employs natural means sometimes to carry out his will."

"Who put the hemlock in the glass?"

"It doesn't matter; Jehovah's will was carried out."

"It matters to the police," Peter reminded him. "Haven't you heard from them yet?"

"I believe they took brother Hershey to the station for questioning."

"Now that David is dead they'll pin a murder charge on him," Peter said.

"The police won't hold brother Hershey for long; worldly authority has ceased," Bruce told him. "In the millennium Christ rules, and we as his servants carry out his orders. God's will is finally being done on Earth, just as Jesus taught us to pray: Thy Kingdom come, they will be done on Earth as it is in heaven."

"I know that spiel by heart ad nauseam," Peter said with a longsuffering tone. "So what are you going to do now: start murdering whoever disagrees with you?"

"Better watch what you print," Bruce answered, and hung up.

But the threat did no good; that evening Bruce read the headline:

| **"King David" Murdered by Religious Sect** |
| --- |

The article stated that Mr. Melvin Hershey had been charged with first-degree murder for poisoning the man whom Jehovah's Watchmen insisted was King David back from the dead. Next to the article was a series of three photographs that Peter had taken. The first photograph was of Hershey wheeling the teacart onto the stage; the second was of David standing next to the teacart, drinking from the glass; the third showed David collapsed on the stage floor.

Another emergency meeting was called to deal with this new problem.

"We must fight this on the grounds of religious freedom," Henderson stated.

"Yes, I think you're right," Cyril agreed. "We know that Jehovah destroyed David for apostasy. It's our religious right to see the matter this way, therefore there was no murder involved, and it's a violation of our religious freedom to try to force us to say that he was murdered."

"Oh, I don't think it's worth our time to try and fight the worldly authorities on this," Bruce said, "They'll be dealt with soon enough by Jehovah, and when they're all destroyed, Jehovah will open the prison doors and Hershey will walk away just like Paul did."

"I agree with brother Kline," Klaus said. "Our biggest concern right now is communicating the truth to the brothers. Let them know that this wasn't a case of murder, but a judgment from Jehovah against apostasy."

"Hmmm," Stingler said, still perusing his copy of the newspaper. "It says here that after the incident hundreds of Watchmen could be seen outside of the auditorium burning their 'No Blood' cards and advance directives."

"So, we'll need to do some damage control on the blood issue," Bruce suggested.

"No," I say we just ignore it," Henderson said. "So what if we lose a few hundred? We have millions of faithful Watchmen who never heard one word of his speech: and they never shall. We preprinted the speech we gave him in the next *Watchman* issue. That will be what is remembered."

"Then how will they know he committed apostasy?" Klaus asked.

"We'll send out another emergency message via the web-site and phone-calls to the branch offices," Cyril said. "We'll just say that he became apostate when he began challenging the blood issue and the authority of the Governing Body, so Jehovah destroyed him in front of thousands of witnesses. Showing that no one is above God's arrangements."

# Layer Three

# 1
## *(Summer, 1971) (Thirty years earlier)*

"David!" Grandma J. called from the basement.

But David, engrossed in his chemistry set, did not answer. He was conducting the fourth step in the third run of his latest experiment, and carefully noting the results in his logbook.

It was when he began the fifth step that he felt a sharp pain in the back of his head, and turned to see Grandma J. hovering over him.

"I've been calling to you for the last five minutes!" She yelled. One hand was fisted on her hip; the other was poised as if to strike him again.

"I didn't hear you," he whimpered.

"Of course not;" she said in a sarcastic tone, "Mr. Jesseson is engrossed in his all-important experiments. He thinks he's going to work for NASA someday, though he's too stupid to wipe his own nose when it's running."

She heaved a long drawn-out sigh and then put both hands on her hips, much to David's relief.

"I need your dirty clothes brought down from upstairs. I had to climb all the stairs up from the basement because Mr. Wizard here is too busy to open his wax-filled ears and listen!"

David jumped up and began running to the stairs.

"Don't run in this house!" she called after him, causing him to change to a rapid pace.

While he was upstairs fetching the laundry hamper, he could hear her presumably talking to herself, but purposely loud enough for him to hear.

"You work and you slave, and do they appreciate it? No. I guess there's no rest for the wicked, and he's my cross to bear. I offer all my suffering up to you, dear Jesus... Where is that boy *now*? He's fast enough when it comes to his foolishness, but give him something important to do—"

As he started back down the stairs, carrying the hamper, she addressed herself directly to him once again. "I'm going to start stepping on your glass vials if you don't hurry up. Crunch, crunch, crunch! Oh, this is fun!"

David began running down the stairs. He tripped on the second to the last step, sending the laundry flying across the room. He landed on his elbows and knees, tearing off the old scab on his left knee, and forming new abrasions on his elbows.

"Didn't I tell you not to run!" Grandma J. hollered, stomping her foot to drive the point home, and accidentally crushing one of David's vials for real this time,

"Good!" She exclaimed with a forced smile. "I'm glad I broke it! Serves you right for running."

"Now clean up this glass," she demanded. "Why should I always be picking up after you?"

David struggled to his feet, and limped over to her. Stooping down he began picking up the glass fragments.

"Not with your *hands*!" She shrieked. "My God, how stupid can you be? You don't pick up broken glass with your *fingers*! I guess I'll have to do it myself before you get more blood on the floor. Look at you, bleeding all over. Why couldn't your mother hang onto her husband and take care of you herself? I'm left cleaning up everybody else's messes.

"I don't have enough to do, now I have to bandage you up too? Come with me to the bathroom and we'll fix your owies."

David obediently followed her to the bathroom where she sprayed antiseptic on his skinned elbows. "Good," she said when he winced.

As she applied bandages she said, "Oh, how I wish you were at least a *normal* child. Why can't you be like Mrs. Donaldson's grandson?"

**2**
*(Fall, 1979) (Eight years later)*

On his way into the dorm party, David heard Angie and Lindsey talking in the kitchen.

"Lin, these guys are all too stupid," Angie whispered.

"I know; they're not going to be any help at all," Lindsey agreed, "we need to meet some of those nerdy types."

"Yeah, too bad smarts and jocks don't go together."

David had been spotted from the living room, and had to move on. As he entered the crowded room, trying to be inconspicuous, he knocked over a stack of magazines that had been precariously balanced on the edge of a bookshelf. Immediately all eyes turned to him.

Randy, the football team's quarterback, called out, "Hey, look what the cat dragged in!"

"Who's *that*?" the young beauty Randy had his arm around said in a tone of utter disgust.

"That's my punching-bag since the seventh-grade," Randy boasted. "Used to kick his ass every day in gym."

"How's the weather up there, Slim?" Jim taunted, shielding his eyes and craning his neck as if David were a hundred feet tall. "I've heard of people with their heads in the clouds, but this is ridiculous!"

"I wish his *face* was in the clouds; then we wouldn't have to look at it!" Randy added with a laugh. "Hey, butt-face, come over her so my girlfriend can watch me flex my muscles squeezing your ugly face off."

David discreetly chose a spot in the opposite corner of the room to sit as the other guys in the room laughed.

"Chicken!" Randy taunted, and then began clucking like one, which made his girlfriend giggle and draw affectionately closer to him.

Angie and Lindsey emerged from the kitchen with the hors d'oeuvre trays.

"Real mature, Randy," Angie said sarcastically, as she set the tray down on the coffee table.

In the awkward moment that followed, as the group made up its collective mind whether Randy's attitude would fall out of favor, or some barb would be hurled in Angie's direction to maintain the juvenile atmosphere, David found himself speaking:

"The semi-pro basketball team I'm trying out for was thinking of having a chicken for a mascot, until I reminded them of the deleterious connotations, of which Randy has so eloquently reminded us.

"It's odd though," he continued, since no one had yet recovered from the shock of hearing a supposedly humiliated wall-flower boldly speak up, and no one had time to think of a witty comeback, "at the same time that ignorant people denigrate the chicken for supposed cowardice, they hold up the male of the species: the rooster, as an icon of bravery and masculinity. Indeed, these birds, in preference to all others, are even trained for illegal cockfight tournaments. Not to mention the fact—with delicate ears in attendance here—that a male chicken: a *cock* is the very same nickname given to the epitome of masculinity: the male organ itself!

"So, thank you, Randy, for complimenting me on my bravery and masculinity," David said with a smile as he looked around the room, gauging the reactions—especially of Angie, "I'll try to continue to live up to it."

"Way to go, man!" Chuck hollered as he leaned forward and gave David a high-five.

"He sure put you in your place," Carl said to Randy with a laugh.

"C'mon, babe," Randy said to his girlfriend, "let's go get us a beer: I don't much like the company here anymore." As he left, Lindsey and Angie came and sat down on either side of David.

"Do you know much about chemistry?" Lindsey asked.

"Or trigonometry?" Angie added.

David smiled, and began chewing one of the little sandwiches Angie offered him from the hors d'oeuvre tray. He was relieved that no one had asked him the name of the imaginary basketball team. His remarkable height evidently led people to believe that even a klutzy intellectual such as himself would be somehow associated with the sport.

**3**
*(Fall, 1987) (Eight years later)*

The professors were seated in a semi-circle in the open area beside the dean's desk, quietly drinking tea. They were using their copies of David's 350-page dissertation as saucers.

David stood before them with his hands clasped behind his back, waiting for their questions. Glancing at the mantle clock, he saw that his presentation had taken the recommended thirty minutes. It had all seemed to go smoothly thus far, but no questions were forthcoming; they just kept sipping tea and sighing. So he took the initiative: "Gentlemen, is there anything I can clarify for you regarding my thesis?"

"You know, it's funny," Professor Morrison said, "you listen to enough of these doctoral defenses and they all begin to sound alike."

"I couldn't make much sense of this one," Professor Adams admitted.

"Sort of incoherent," Professor Williams said with a chuckle.

"Listen son," Professor Morrison said, "why don't you just tell us what it's all about in plain English."

"What's it all about, Alfie?" Professor James sang as he glanced out the window.

"Yes," Professor Adams added, "and what is it that your view contributes to the field of philosophy?" He held up the thesis and asked, "What's *new* in all of this?"

It was then that David realized that he had succeeded a little too well in sounding just like these old professors; even *they* couldn't understand him.

"In brief, it is a new answer to Solipsism, or radical skepticism."

"Define those terms," Professor Morrison demanded.

"*Solipsism* is the view that the world is just a thought in the thinker's head and has no objective reality: the thinker is the only existing entity. *Radical skepticism* is the idea that we cannot know anything."

"And what is your answer to these viewpoints?" Professor Williams asked.

"If it were true, then I would be living in the best of all possible worlds: the one invented by myself for myself."

"Ah," Professor Morrison remarked, "and then you can level all of Voltaire's arguments in *Candide* against Leibniz and his *Tout est pour le mieux dans le meilleur des mondes possibles.*"

"Yes, but what's new about that?" Adams demanded.

"It's more than that," David replied. "All of my life I've been capable of lucid dreaming."

"*Lurid* dreams?" Williams asked in a shocked tone.

"No, not lurid, *lucid,*" Morrison explained.

"Define the term." Williams asked.

"The conscious awareness that one is dreaming, and the subsequent ability to influence the content of one's dream," David responded.

"The relevance?" Williams asked.

"Well, it's not a difficult skill to learn for most people. As my research shows, within thirty days I was able to successfully teach the majority of fellow students who volunteered for the study."

"Relevance to your *thesis*, Jesseson?" Williams demanded.

"Solipsists have always answered the challenge as to why their imagined world is not perfect by saying that this is the best world their mind is capable of imagining without being bored.

"But lucid dreaming provides the counterpoint. It shows that the mind can easily imagine a better, and more exciting world.

"If people can easily control their dreams once they know that they are dreaming, and can then dream about what they desire: driving a fast car; sun-bathing on a deserted beach; having sex with whomever they most desire; a world without war, pain or death, and so on and so on, as my thesis details— Then a solipsist, believing life to be his or her own thoughts, should automatically experience a perfect life: having everything they want, with no pain, disappointment, or sadness.

"Such a perfect world would not be limited to dreams (that state where the mind takes over independent of reality) if our conscious state itself is just the mind independent of a (non-existent) reality, as the solipsist view holds that it is.

"But instead of this, we find the exact opposite happens in real life. Instead of life conforming to our ideal, we conform to the ideals of others.

"Here I am, gentlemen, as a case in point: standing in a room full of professors, trying my damnedest to sound like a professor in order to win your approval."

"And what would you rather be doing, if solipsism were true, and this was like one of your lucid dreams?" Adams asked.

"Well, let's just say that you wouldn't be males, and you would be more, shall we say, *friendly*," David said with a mischievous grin, which brought forth a like response from Professor James.

But a stern look crossed Professor William's face as he said: "So, if you created the world (as Solipsism contends that you did) it would be a world without professors such as we?"

"If I ruled the world, every day would be the first day of spring—" Professor James sang, feebly snapping his fingers.

"I wouldn't necessarily say that," David replied, "but maybe this would be a less difficult experience: maybe you'd have all jumped up when I finished my presentation and shook my hand and slapped me on the back."

"Or given you a standing ovation?" Professor James asked.

"But that's not a complete representation of solipsism," Professor Morrison said. "Have you forgotten about the 'brain in the vat' thought experiment? That holds that the mind is not the source of the world it imagines, but rather something external creates the world in the mind. Some call this God."

"But why," David replied, "would the external source also create the illusion of dreaming, not to mention lucid dreaming? The owners of the 'brain in the vat' would surely have some reason: some motivation for going to all the trouble of creating an imaginary world for the brain to think about. Why then, give it states of unconsciousness interspersed with nonsensical dreams? What could they hope to learn from this?"

"A solipsist would say," Professor Morrison replied, "that the mind simply does not know, and cannot be expected to understand the reasoning that goes on beyond the confines of its imaginary world. Sleep and dreams, just like every other experience, are just illusions that the brain is subjected to via the external force."

"And you know, of course," Professor Adams began, "that solipsism is not falsifiable. Therefore, I don't have to read it to know that your thesis cannot possibly disprove the notion."

"At the same time," Professor Morrison added, "solipsism can never be considered scientific for the very reason that it cannot be falsified."

"Nor can any philosophical viewpoint," Professor James reminded them. "All we can hope to do is to accumulate reasons as to why such a view would be unlikely. In reality that's all that science can ever do. This thesis, I believe, admirably accomplishes that goal, adding another forceful reason against the likelihood of solipsism."

David didn't know what to say anymore, and just smiled. He noticed that the professors were all paging through his thesis with renewed interest; evidently looking for the descriptions of the more lurid lucid dreams. This told him that they had not bothered to read it before now: they had probably just read the abstract and skimmed through the rest of it.

After several minutes of silent reading, Professor Morrison looked up and said, "Well, in any case, you seem to have set solipsism on its head, Jesseson."

"Upon further review, I do believe this is a well-researched, first-class work," Professor Adams concluded.

"Gentlemen," Professor James said with a conspiratorial wink to the others, "shall we?"

Smiles actually appeared on the professor's faces, and they jumped to their feet, rushed over and congratulated David.

"Now, if this scene isn't a positive proof of solipsism," Professor James said as he shook David's hand and slapped him on the back, "I don't know what is!"

"No, don't listen to him, Jesseson," Professor Morrison said with a chuckle, "*Il faut cultiver notre jardin!*"

**4**
*(Winter, 1996) (Nine years later)*

David smiled and wrote a large red A on the top of the exam paper, set it aside, and picked up the next one from the stack on his desk.

Sarah ran into the room and said: "Mom says you're to come downstairs for the inner-view now."

"*Interview*, Sarah," he corrected. "Tell her I'll be right down."

"In-ter-view," she repeated to herself as she ran out of the room.

He checked his appointment-book for the day: "Let's see, 2:30 interview with free-lance reporter: dress for pictures."

Standing up, he pulled off his vest as he walked towards the bedroom closet.

Five minutes later he was dressed in a white tunic, sitting on the living room couch beside his wife, Ann, answering questions from a wiry young Peter Frawley.

"When did you start dressing up as Socrates?"

"It was about eight years ago. I had just gotten my professorship, and I was having trouble getting the students interested in what I was saying. Basically, I was reciting facts to them: Socrates was born in 469 BCE, died in 399 BCE from hemlock poisoning (after being condemned to death on the charge of corrupting the youth and introducing new gods.) And so on.

"The students would start yawning at about that point. That really bothered me, because to me philosophy is vitally interesting, and I wanted to share my enthusiasm with them: but I wasn't reaching them.

"Then I happened to be going through my closet: throwing out old things, when I spotted this white tunic I had worn to the dean's masquerade ball a few months earlier, and it made me think that one way to make philosophy come alive for the students would be to make Socrates come alive. So, I took a chance, and instead of their boring Professor Jesseson, my students were surprised to find Socrates teaching them the following day.

"And it worked; I—or I should say Socrates—had their rapt attention. They were asking him questions, and responding to his questions. It was great. And my class become very popular."

"That's what attracted me to him," Ann said. "I was in that first class of his. I thought that any professor willing to risk making a fool of himself was worth getting to know better."

"We were married a year later." David added.

"And then, along came Sarah," Ann said, taking David's hand.

"And today, I understand you—as Socrates—are a frequent guest speaker at universities all across the country?" Peter asked.

"Yes, I've been asked to speak as Socrates numerous times over the years. It seems to increase enrollment, or at least enthusiasm for philosophy courses."

Peter next turned to Ann, who had been half engrossed in a crossword puzzle.

"And what about you, Mrs. Jesseson? How do you feel about your husband dressing up like this and play-acting?"

"Oh, it's been wonderful for his ego. All philosophy students love Socrates."

"Yes, thank you," Peter said, leaning forward, "but that's not what I asked you. How does it make *you* feel?"

Startled to realize that someone was actually interested in her opinion, Ann set aside her puzzle and looked nervously at David.

"It's all right, my dear," David assured her, "tell him what you really think."

"Mr. Frawley," she said, "did you ever see that Woody Allen movie *Zelig*?"

David stirred uncomfortably in his seat.

"No ma'am," Peter replied, "I'm afraid I missed that one."

"In that movie," Ann explained, "Woody Allen plays the 'chameleon man': a man who adapts to whatever company he finds himself in. If he's with overweight bearded men, within a few minutes he's got a bloated belly and whiskers. If he's with a psychiatrist, he starts behaving like a psychiatrist, and actually believes that he has a practice, etc. You get the idea?"

"Yes, most amusing."

"It's *not*, Mr. Frawley, I assure you," Ann replied. "Not if you have to live with it day in and day out."

An awkward moment passed. Finally, Ann resumed her crossword puzzle, and David stood up.

"Can I see you to the door, Mr. Frawley?" he asked.

"Of course, thank you both so much. I'm sure my readers will be most enlightened."

As they were walking down the hall, David spoke quietly to Peter: "I'm afraid my wife feels that I lose my own personality when I put on this garb. Although it may have initially attracted her to me, she now wishes I were a little less eccentric and more like the other professors."

"I understand, it must be hard for her when you travel."

"What I really would like to be is a reporter like you," David said. "Asking people questions, getting the story, and then writing it up to present to the world. That's the life! You know, it's not so different from what I do. Maybe I'll come to your place sometime, pencil and notebook in hand, and interview you. What do you say?"

"A most amusing idea, I'm sure."

"David!" Ann called from the living room.

"But I hear Mrs. Jesseson calling you, so I'd best take my leave now."

"Very well," David said, opening the door.

As Peter walked out, David whispered: "You don't happen to have an extra notebook and pencil on you by any chance do you?"

"I'm afraid not, good-day!" Peter said and strode off to his car without looking back.

**5**
*(September 2, 2001) (Five years later)*

David had been going over it in his mind all night.

As he took his morning shower he went over it again.

How had it all gone so wrong? Ann insisted that he no longer had a personality of his own—or maybe never had one to begin with. She refused to speak to him anymore after the divorce. He was not allowed unsupervised contact with Sarah.

Much to his surprise, the university had readily, almost gratefully, accepted his resignation. Now he had followed Ann and Sarah out to San Diego, determined to introduce himself back into their lives, and become a family again. But when he called her apartment he heard a male voice, and hung up. Had Ann found someone else already in these past few months? Someone who was a 'real person': as she claimed he never was?

Tomorrow he would arrange to bump into Sarah on her way home from her new high school. He would need her as an intermediary to win his way back into Ann's heart. Such assertiveness would show her that he indeed possessed a personality of his own.

But what could he do to get through this day? The anticipation—the bottled-up energy—was driving him crazy.

Hanging in his closet was the one thing that always brought him solace.

The students at San Diego University would be unpacking, and then milling about, waiting for tomorrow and the start of the school year. They'd be ripe for a visit from Socrates. He could talk to them about education and life in general.

Ann need never know.

He donned the tunic, and headed out.

As soon as he entered the campus grounds and saw students in the distance, he once again felt at home.

But, before he could reach them, a car pulled up alongside him, and two large black men jumped out of the back and grabbed his arms on either side. The one on the left said, "Listen man, we all want you to come to our dorm and talk to the brothers; they're all homesick and everything."

"Oh, I can walk," David said in surprise, trying to pull free.

The man on his right struck David in the back of the head with a billy club, rendering him unconscious. Then they shoved him into the backseat and sped off.

"Man, this hazing thing is going too far," said the one on the left, with a laugh, as if he'd made a particularly witty remark.

"Shut the hell up," said the one on the right. "You just trying to confuse me; hazing was the story for our *last* gig. Anyway, dude's still breathing. He's gonna be all right."

"You both shut-up," said the muscular white driver. "Ain't nothin' but some homeless white trash, anyway. Just help me watch the time."

# Layer Four

# 1

*(Summer, 1992) (Nine years earlier) (Queens, New York)*

"I don't think anyone's home here either," elder Johnson remarked, picking up the leather book-bag he had set at their feet while they had waited.

Peter followed him along the sidewalk and back to his car. He was tired, and he hoped elder Johnson didn't have any more addresses written on his "not-at-home" list.

"Well, that was the last one on the list," elder Johnson said as put the car in drive. "Thanks for coming out in service today, and helping me work my 'not-at-homes.'"

"No problem," Peter replied.

"I only wish you could be out here *every* Saturday, along with your father and brother." Peter had all he could do to suppress a long-suffering sigh as the all too familiar lecture began.

"Your father works five days a week. He should give it a rest on the weekends, and join in Jehovah's service, along with *both* of his boys. Otherwise, it seems he's just pursuing material gain instead of performing his Scriptural duties."

Peter's twin brother, Paul, had gone with their father tree-trimming that weekend.

In order to make ends meet, their father worked five days a week for a tree-trimming service, and then on Saturdays he rented the equipment from his boss and did his own free-lance work. Ever since they turned 14, three months ago, Peter and Paul took turns working with him on Saturdays while the other one went out in service.

Truth to tell, their father would rather have had both of them helping him, but he had made this concession to the elders, who had complained to him on several occasions about the paltry number of field-service hours the family turned in every month.

As elder Johnson drove him home, Peter smiled to himself as he contemplated that it would be his turn next week. He and his brother were the "tree monkeys:" clambering up the trunks and scooting out on the branches, with a chainsaw hooked to their tool-belts. Their father told them where to cut, ran the chipper, and negotiated with the homeowners.

At last they had arrived at Peter's home. For some reason, elder Johnson pulled into the alley to drop him off. "Thanks for driving," Peter said. "See you tomorrow."

"Not so fast," the elder said. Grabbing the sleeve of Peter's sport coat, he pulled him close, leaned over, and kissed him on the mouth.

Peter was so surprised that he didn't notice at first the feel of the elder's hand rubbing his crotch.

Peter pulled his face away, but the elder held tight to his sleeve.

"This time open your mouth," elder Johnson instructed him. "Be agape for agapé: the Christian love fest!"

"Stop it!" Peter cried, turning his head away, so that the elder got a mouthful of hair.

Peter squirmed away, but the elder hit the power lock on the door, and Peter was momentarily trapped.

"Don't look so shocked; I forgot and thought you were Paul. Believe me; he lets me do much more. Which one of you do you suppose I will recommend to be made a Ministerial Servant first?"

Peter frantically tried all the buttons on the door until one caused the door to unlock with a muffled click. He threw his shoulder into the door and fell onto the blacktop. Scrambling to his feet, he ran into the house. He didn't look back until he was safely inside. Then he saw elder Johnson slowly moving around the front of the car. Peter made a quick visual check to make sure the door was dead bolted. But the elder didn't attempt to come in; he just slammed the car door, and then walked back around to the driver's side, got in, smiled at himself in his rearview mirror, and drove off.

*

Meanwhile, halfway across town, Paul was also smiling. He was straddling a large branch on a catalpa tree, about thirty-feet up, and gazing down at the children who were watching him from the safety of the sidewalk in front of the client's house. Amongst them was a girl he recognized from school.

His father was in the driveway, engrossed in feeding a large branch into the chipper.

There were several "sucker branches" shooting out from the limb about eight feet over Paul's head. He knew his father would ask him to cut these next.

Paul decided to impress the girl. Removing the safety harness, he stood up on the branch he had been straddling. Then he took the safety off the chainsaw, lifted it up over his head, and squeezed the trigger. The electric ignition kicked in, and with his well-practiced moves the branches began falling on either side of him.

There was one sucker branch slightly beyond reach, so Paul took a step closer to it, leaned forward, and stretched himself to the limit. With his finger on the trigger he couldn't quite reach the branch, so he locked it into the On position and held it by the base. This did the trick: the teeth of the chainsaw began biting into the branch.

But the branch he was standing on was a little wet, and his foot slipped causing him to lose his balance. He dropped the chainsaw as he tried to regain his balance, and it roared past him in its descent to the ground, ripping into his chest and thighs. Jerking back in a reflex of pain he fell backwards out of the tree, and plunged to the ground. The chainsaw landed first: the impact stopping it before Paul fell on top of it, breaking his ribs and splitting his skull open.

**2**
*(September 4, 2000) (Eight years later)*

Peter was checking the police reports, as he did every morning, looking for potential stories, when it caught his eye. A woman had phoned in a complaint of harassment by 'some religious nut'.

He quickly looked up the phone number, spoke briefly with the woman, and was granted an interview.

He poked his head into his boss's office and announced, "I'm on my way to check out a story."

"What about?"

"Harassment and freedom of religion."

"Good stuff! Let me know what you find."

Peter grabbed his camera, rushed out of the building and hopped into his ancient Volkswagen "bug". He still felt a rush of adrenaline when he was in pursuit of a possible story. As usual, this surge of energy was frustrated by heavy traffic. It was a good hour before he arrived, and he needed to take several deep breaths to calm himself down before he left his car.

He took out his notebook and double-checked the address: 4440 Braeburn Road. "This must be the place," he muttered to himself.

A pretty young woman with short black hair, dressed in a white blouse and immaculately clean white jeans, answered the door. She looked to be in her early twenties: about Peter's age.

"Peter Frawley, from the *San Diego Reader*," he said by way of introduction.

"Hi, I'm Mary Snow," she said, lightly taking his hand, "please come in."

She led him into what he took to be the "drawing room". It was spacious and contained expensive looking furniture. Huge paintings in golden frames hung in profusion on the white walls. A grand piano, with its hood open, stood in front of the bay windows that jutted out onto a view of a rock and cactus garden.

Peter looked down at the white carpet and noticed that Mary's bare feet were half lost in its thick white shag. He immediately kicked off his loafers.

"Please sit," she said, indicating the large overstuffed sofa.

"Thank you," Peter said. "Nice place you've got here."

"Thanks. It's home," she smiled.

"Do you live here all by yourself?"

"Just me and my roommate, Jenny, ever since my folks died."

"And did Jenny witness the alleged harassment?"

"No, she was at work."

"Can you tell me exactly what happened?"

"It's happened several times. But this most recent time was the proverbial last straw."

"Please tell me about it."

"Well, this guy—must be in his sixties—he keeps coming by and wanting to come in. He says he's some kind of a watchman and he used to play here as a kid or something. Anyway, the guy gives me the creeps. So I told him no, that I didn't feel comfortable letting him in the house."

"And how many times has he come by?"

"This was the fourth time. It seems to happens every year about this time."

"And what made this time the 'last straw'?"

"Well, when he saw he wasn't getting anywhere with me, he took out a Bible and started preaching at me."

"Oh," Peter said, with a look of recognition. "Did he say he was a *Jehovah's Watchman* by any chance?"

"Yes, that sounds about right.

"You'd think that telling someone No *once* would be enough, wouldn't you?" she asked. "After that it's harassment. That's what I've always been told."

"You're right."

"Anyway, he said this was a special house because one of their leaders lived and died here, and they had certain beliefs about this house, so it was part of his religious heritage, and I was denying him his religious freedom by keeping him out! Can you believe that?"

"It's a strange world," Peter agreed.

"But where are my manners?" she said. "Do you want a drink?"

"I would love a drink, thank you."

A minute later she reemerged from the kitchen with two tall glasses of lemonade.

"Are you going to write about this?" she asked, handing him his glass.

"I don't know," he teased, "it would have to be an extraordinarily good glass of lemonade to merit its own story."

"Not the lemonade, silly," she laughed.

"Yes, I think I could write about this," he said seriously, "but right now it's a very short story: little more than a paragraph, really. I'd like to get some more background, to sort of flesh it out."

"Well, I have to give a piano lesson in a few minutes," she said. "But I'm free this evening."

"Great! I know a little Italian restaurant not far from here. Would you consider filling me in over dinner?"

"Sort of an 'I'll fill you *in* if you'll fill me *up*' deal?" she asked.

"Exactly!" he said with a smile.

"Can Jenny come too?" she asked, "She doesn't get out much."

"Sort of a 'two for one' deal?" Peter asked, and then wished he hadn't. "No problem; the more the merrier!" A journalist falling back on a cliché is inexcusable, he thought to himself. Worse than that, it still sounded like he was anticipating some sort of a ménage à trois

She smiled, and he took it as being amused by his nervousness. But in reality she was savoring the disappointment she read in his eyes over being chaperoned by her roommate.

**3**
*(December 4, 2000) (Three months later)*

"This is a very special day," Peter told Mary when she looked surprised at his ordering two glasses of white wine.

"Is it?" she asked, feigning ignorance as she studied the menu. It was too much to hope that he would be thinking the same thing she was. She decided to keep quiet and let him announce what he thought was so special about the day.

The wine arrived and they waited in silence as the waiter filled their glasses without waiting for the tasting ritual.

When they were alone again, Peter lifted his glass towards her and proclaimed, "A toast!"

Mary lifted her glass and delicately touched it to his with a scarcely audible clink.

He gazed into her eyes and smiled. "To us, on our three-month anniversary."

A warm feeling rushed into her as she took a sip, but it wasn't from the wine. Her pretended disinterest could no longer be maintained, and she broke into a huge, beautiful smile.

"I'm very happy," she said. "I know I should say something more profound—"

"No," he said, "don't apologize; nothing is more profound than happiness."

They each took another sip of wine, and then held hands across the table in silent contemplation for a while.

"Christmas is three weeks away," she sighed, "but I have a confession to make."

"They say it's good for the soul," he said in an encouraging way, but he was looking at his glass of wine at the time, so she wasn't sure if he meant confession or wine.

"I'm broke," she admitted, with a nervous giggle. "I wanted to get you something nice for Christmas, but I'm so financially strapped that I simply can't manage it."

"It's all right," Peter said, "Christmas isn't at all important to me. We never had Christmas when I was growing up."

"How sad! Christmas was always a big to-do in our family. If my folks were still alive I'd be asking you to have Christmas with them. We've been going together three months, and I'd certainly have wanted them to meet you by now."

He knew she was hinting about his taking her to meet *his* family, so he tried changing the subject. "I'm sorry to hear about your financial difficulties."

"Oh, they're worse than you can imagine," she said.

"But you've got so many nice things, and such a big house," he said, puzzled.

"Those are all things my father left me: along with his massive debts. He was addicted to gambling, and owed far more than what it's all worth."

"Why don't you declare bankruptcy and make a new start?"

Mary hesitated, idly shifting her silverware around while she decided if she should reveal more. Peter watched her in patient silence. When she looked up at him he gave her an understanding smile.

"I'm afraid," she said quietly, "a little thing like bankruptcy won't deter the sort of men my father owed money to."

"I see," he said. "What can I do to help?"

"I've told you too much already," she sighed. "It's better you don't know about that part of my life—I don't want to see you get hurt."

"Hey, haven't you noticed?" he asked, "you're part of my life now. This is one of those 'you jump: I jump' deals."

She smiled, but then turned serious and said, "I just don't want to see it become one of those 'I get shot: you get shot' deals. There's no reason to drag you down with me into this mess. These guys don't play around."

"Maybe I can help pull you up somehow," he offered.

"Why should you? It's not like we're married—"

"No, don't say that;" he said with an earnestness that surprised her. "It's *exactly* like we're married. I consider this relationship one of those 'for better or for worse' deals."

"The guy's just bleeding me dry," she said. He noticed that her chin was quivering. He had never seen her cry before.

"My father owed him millions, so he's taking all the money I make every month just to pay a little towards the interest. I'm giving him all I have, and I'm still just getting deeper into debt. I keep having to raise Jenny's rent to the point that she's threatening to walk out on me; and I don't blame her." She took a tissue out of her purse and wiped her eyes and nose. "And now I'm afraid you'll leave me too."

"I will never leave you," he said, taking her hand again. "Having debts that you didn't even make: that's not a moral failure. What sort of a person would leave someone for something like that?"

"So you would leave me only for a moral failure?" she asked, a little apprehensively.

"Listen," he said, "you don't even know what moral failure is. You should hear about *my* life. Then I'd wonder if you were going to leave *me*."

"Peter, you're the most honest, morally upright person I've ever known."

"You don't know what my life has been like," he said.

"Tell me," she pleaded. "I've opened up and told you my dark secret."

"All right," he said, surprising himself at how much he had come to trust her.

"I've never told anyone about this—well, not all of it, anyway."

"Have either of you saved room for desert?" the waiter asked.

Annoyed by the interruption, they both waved him away in mute reply.

"Tell *me*," she asked, looking deep into Peter's eyes.

"I know you've been wondering about my family, and why I don't take you to see them."

She nodded, her eyes forming an expectant look.

"My father is the only one still living. My mother died when Paul and I were still babies. Paul was my twin brother: he died when I was fourteen."

"I'm sorry," she said. "I didn't know you were a twin. That must've been very hard on you: growing up without a mother's love, and then losing your twin brother so young."

"Yes, it was. My father couldn't handle it. He attempted suicide, failed, and became catatonic. He's in an institution now, he doesn't know me, so I don't bother visiting him anymore; what's the point?"

"Oh, Peter. I had no idea!"

"That's not all," Peter said. "It's the *way* they died: senselessly, needlessly.

"You see, the whole family was involved with a religious cult: the Jehovah's Watchmen."

"Oh," she said in surprise, "like that creep that comes to my house: the one who brought us together."

"Yes. Well, you see they used to believe that organ transplants were a sin. My mother needed a kidney transplant, and they had a suitable donor organ all lined up and everything, but because of her religious beliefs she refused it... and she died.

"Then, my brother had a terrible accident, and he needed blood. Well, the Watchmen believe to this day that blood transfusions are a sin. So my father refused to let him have any blood... and he died.

"That was bad. Really bad. My father went into a deep depression. But what finally drove him over the edge—" Peter's voice broke, and he took a moment, gazing out the window to collect himself.

"Go on, Peter," she said, "it's best to let it all out."

He took a sip of wine, sighed, and then looking her intently in the eyes, continued: "You see, this religion has a magazine called *Arise!* and in 1994 they published an article entitled *"Youth Who Put God First"*. That article featured 26 young people who had lost their lives by refusing blood transfusions: my brother was one of them.

"Had they asked your father permission to include your brother's name in the article?"

Peter laughed sardonically. "Permission? Hell no! Here was something that was so personal, and so tormenting to my father and me, and they just *used* it. Used our personal tragedy to promote their religion: 'look how great we are, we can even convince parents to let their children *die* just because we tell them to!'"

"What drove my father mad eventually drove me to a life of crime. After he was committed I was adopted by an elder from our congregation: an elder who had molested Paul before he died, and who had once tried molesting me!"

"Didn't you report him?"

"I tried, but they had this rule that the molesting has to be witnessed by two or three people—like the Bible says—before they'll take any action. So I wasn't believed, and the elder continued in good standing!

"I started hiding a knife under my pillow at night.

"It was an impossible situation: living in constant fear. I ended up running away when I was fifteen.

"I lived on the streets of L.A., and got involved in petty crime in order to survive. I can justify it, but it's not something I'm proud of. It was the low point of my life.

"I had been in and out of jail several times when a social worker named Christine made me her pet project. She saw that I liked to write things down, so she got me enrolled in a journalism class at the junior college.

"I really got into that. It's like I'd finally found what I was cut out to do. And our instructor was just terrific. She really made the subject come alive. One time she even came to school dressed as the old-time reporter Nelly Bly, and told us how she went out and *made* news to report on.

"It turned my life around, and eventually I got lucky and landed this job at the *San Diego Reader*. And that's how I met you: pursuing a story. And the rest, as they say, is history."

Mary pushed back her chair, stood up, walked over to his side of the table, and sat down on his lap. Putting her arms around him, she kissed him on the cheek. "Thank you for telling me," she whispered. "It makes me love you all the more. I'm so glad we found each other. We're each other's saviors."

## 4
*(September 1, 2001) (Nine months later)*

Mary and Jenny were both gone for the weekend, leaving Peter to watch the house. He had decided to surprise them (and alleviate his boredom) by putting a fresh coat of paint on the kitchen walls.

He was just starting to pry the lid off of the first paint can when the doorbell interrupted him.

He slipped the screwdriver into the back pocket of his jeans. Then he chased Jenny's house-cat into the bathroom and shut the door. 'Whiskers' was an indoor cat, and would be helpless in her naiveté if she ever found herself outside.

When he finally opened the front door he saw two neatly dressed, but badly scarred men squinting at him. Peter guessed that they were in their late thirties.

"Mary home?" the lanky one asked, and then took a long drag from his cigarette.

"No, I'm sorry she's not."

"Who the hell are you?" he asked as he flicked the cigarette into the cactus garden.

"Might I ask you the same question, first?" Peter made bold to ask.

"I'm Mr. Laurel, and this here," he said, motioning to the silent bulk of a man standing beside him, "this here is my good friend Mr. Hardy."

"Well, Laurel and Hardy, I'm Mary's fiancé, so if there's any business you have with her, you can tell me, without all the funny stuff."

"Well, you know their old movies can make you laugh so hard you cry. And by the time we leave you just might be crying yourself." At this he nodded to the bulk, who forced his way through the door, and knocked Peter onto the floor, allowing the lanky one to stride in and shut the door behind him.

"You'll have to excuse my associate, Mr. Hardy; he's had a bad day. You see, yesterday—Friday—was his payday, and I wasn't able to pay him. And do you know why?"

"I wouldn't hazard a guess," Peter said, picking himself up off the floor.

"It's because I'm broke. And do you know why? It's because of your girlfriend: Mary. She owes me beau coup bucks. But does she pay me?"

"She's been paying you all that she can."

"Has she now?" he asked, and nodded to his sidekick again, who threw Peter back onto the floor.

"Seems to me if she has a second source of income from a well-paid up-and-coming young reporter, she should start paying me more every month. That would keep Mr. Hardy happy, and you off the floor—or worse. Because if Mr. Hardy is happy, then everyone is happy. But if Mr. Hardy is hurting, then everyone is hurting."

"Look," Peter said, "I'm not afraid to call the police. We have surveillance cameras capturing this entire scene, you know."

"Oh, I'm not afraid to call them either," he replied with calm confidence. "You know my brother? He's practically the chief of police. I can call him for you right now, and have him come over if you like. But he'll just want a cut of his own."

"What if we paid you off completely? Would that get you out of our lives?"

"Of course! You don't think I enjoy spending my time pestering people for what's owed me, do you? I'm a reasonable man. I just want what's coming to me."

"How much does she owe you now?"

"You mean how much do the *two of you* owe me, now. Let's see, today it's six and a half million. Tomorrow—who knows, with today's interest rates, inflation and all? I think it's going up a thousand a day, isn't that right, Mr. Hardy?"

His companion grunted in reply, and grimaced in what Peter took for an attempt at a smile.

Peter took the screwdriver out of his back pocket and held it menacingly towards his assailants before getting to his feet again. "I'm more streetwise than you think," he said. "I've spent time in jail, and I've learned how to take care of myself—and those I love—one way or another."

The lanky one eyed the weapon, smirked, and said, "You know what I think I'll do, just to show you what a generous, patient guy I am? I think I'll leave Mary alone for a while: give her a vacation from her payments, just like your major credit card companies sometimes do. I'll just collect the thousand in interest from *you* every day until you can't pay me no more. What d'ya think of that, Mr. big shot?

"I'll even give you 24 hours to come up with the first grand.

"Now my associate and I are going to take our leave. And if you try to use that screwdriver on anything besides screws, we'll drive it so far up your ass that it'll poke out your nostrils."

With that the men walked out the door. Peter stood staring at it for a full minute: his body oozing with outrage and frustration. Finally, he found some measure of solace from the liquor cabinet.

He gave up on the painting. He poured himself a second drink and sat on the piano bench, thumping out the few chords Mary had taught him. He glanced at the sheet music staring him in the face: *Chopin's Polonaise Opus 53*: subtitled *"The Heroic"*. It was her favorite piece, and it had become his as well, ever since she first played it for him. But now it made him scoff; he was feeling anything but heroic.

There was no earthly way he could ever raise the kind of money that would satisfy these men. He wouldn't be able to rescue Mary from them. And what little money Mary earned from her piano recitals and teaching wouldn't keep them at bay much longer, even with Jenny's rent and Peter's salary helping out.

Frustrated, he turned his mind to his work. He had an interview scheduled the next day at the university as part of his piece on out-of-control hazing in the new fraternities. He sat at his desk and began reviewing his notes.

At nine pm he was startled awake by the phone. Straightening up from the desk, he heard the answering machine kick in.

"Hi, this is Mary and Jenny!" Mary's cheerful, recorded voice announced, "You know what to do, so wait for the beep, and tell us what's on your mind!"

Then came a man's voice, authoritative, yet slightly hesitant: "Uh, yes, MS Snow, this is brother—I mean *Mister* Kline. I was at your place last year about this time, and evidently we had a bit of a misunderstanding.

"I just want you to know that I'll be in the neighborhood again tomorrow, and after what happened the last time I don't intend to come knocking on your door. But I *do* intend to sit in my car on the public street and reminisce a little, while I look at Beth-Sarim—I mean your house.

"So don't get excited and call the police or accuse me of violating any restraining order. I'm giving you fair notice of my intentions, which are well within the law. I'll be there at precisely 7:45 am, and I will be gone no later than 8:00 am. Thank you for your understanding."

"Beth-Sarim," Peter repeated to himself, with a laugh. He had investigated the history of the house a year ago when he was trying to make Mary's experience into a story. The story was rejected, and he hadn't thought about it again until this phone call. "What idiots we all were." He said, recalling his beliefs when he was with the Watchmen.

Then he staggered into Mary's bedroom and set the alarm clock for 6:00 am: plenty of time to get up and make his 7:00 appointment, and be long gone from the house before the creepy Watchman came to stare at it.

**5**
*(September 2, 2001) (The next day)*

"And are all of your members black?" Peter asked the Alpha Beta Sigma fraternity president and vice-president: Joel Grey and Ramsees Mason.

"Well, yeah. Just like all the ones in the Phi Beta Kappa are white," Joel replied. "So, what's that prove? If we're racist, then so are they."

Peter saw in his notes that a professor had told him that their fraternity letters really stood for All Black Students, but from the defensiveness in the young man's voice, he decided not to pursue this.

The weather was so nice that morning that they had decided to hold the interview outdoors on the steps leading to one of the dorms. Peter enjoyed looking at the clear blue sky, and breathing the cool, relatively fresh air, but his butt was getting sore from the cement step.

"And what sorts of initiation rites do your prospective members have to go through?" he asked, cutting to the chase.

As the two young men struggled to find an evasive answer, Peter spotted "Laurel and Hardy" approaching.

"I'm sorry, I'm going to have to cut this short," Peter said, "these two guys headed our way are trouble. I'll call you."

But as he stood to go they grabbed his arms and held him down. "Best just stay put," Joel said.

"I see you've met my boys," 'Laurel' said, "You see: I have contacts everywhere."

He lit a cigarette, coughed for a good minute, spat, and finally said: "Set him up on his feet, boys."

After Peter had been pulled to his feet, 'Laurel' took a drag on his cigarette, and exhaled the poisonous fumes into Peter's face, asking: "You got my money?"

"No, I don't." Peter replied, trying not to sound frightened.

"Too bad. I thought you were smarter than that," 'Laurel' said, pulling a switchblade from his back pocket. "A thousand bucks don't buy much anymore these days. But I'm gonna be generous once again, and give you that much for just one of your fingers."

Peter's first thought was that a switchblade was a poor choice for such a task. He doubted that it would be able to cut through the bone. The man was probably bluffing. Even so, this was getting ridiculous. Somehow this man knew way too much about Peter: he realized he'd have to be smarter in his dealings with these men.

"Any preference?" 'Laurel' asked, waving the knife at Peter's fingers.

"Yeah, this one!" Peter said, jerking his right arm free and pointing his middle finger defiantly in his tormentor's face.

"Let him go, boys," 'Laurel' said, shaking his head in mock regret. "This one's too dumb to be scared; thinks he's some kinda hero or something. We'll just pay a visit on his fiancé instead. Her fingers are prettier anyway."

Then Peter spotted something even more out of place than the scene they were presenting: David Jesseson, whom he'd interviewed years before, dressed in his white tunic, slowly walking towards a group of students seated around a picnic table in the far distance.

"Wait!" Peter yelled.

"There's only one thing that'll make me wait, and it's green." 'Laurel' said with a smirk.

"How about if I pay you the full six and a half million before the year is up?"

"How are you gonna come up with that kind of money? Rob a bank?"

"Sort of, but I'll need your help for just a few minutes."

"The boy's got a plan! I told you boys he was smart. What do you need?"

"You see that guy over there in white?"

"The nut case in the white sheet? What about him?"

"What time is it?" Peter asked urgently.

"It's nearly half-past seven."

"We have to act fast, or the whole deal is off! Have your 'boys' take that guy to Mary's house right now! They've got to drop him off outside the house before 7:45, and then they need to high-tail it out of there."

"That's it?"

"Yes! I'll take care of the rest, but have them go right *now*: it's worth millions if they can drop him there and leave before 7:45."

**6**
*(September 3, 2001) (The next day)*

"These people have been desperately waiting for King David to show up," Peter told David in his room at the Hotel Margaret. "You are their dream come true!"

David sat on the bed and made no response.

"Here," Peter said, rummaging through his suitcase. He pulled out a large, thick blue book and plopped it on the bed beside David.

"*Aid to Bible Understanding*," David read the title absently.

"There's an article in this book all about David," Peter explained. "It's everything they think they know about him—I mean about *you*."

"Yes?" David said, unsure of what Peter expected him to do with this information.

"Well, you should read it over for—uh—*accuracy*. This is how they have thought of you, so if anything's wrong you should know about it so you can set them straight about your life."

"But," David began hesitantly, "I'm somewhat confused. You see, I thought—I think I might be Socrates, not David."

"No," Peter said sternly, "that was a mistake. Remember what your therapist told you about that?" Taking a hopeful guess that David had seen a therapist who told him something useful.

"He said I was David, not Socrates," David replied firmly.

"That's right, you're David: you know it, and they know it. No one here needs Socrates; they need David—or maybe a David who *thinks* like Socrates."

Peter opened the nightstand drawer and pulled out a Gideon Bible.

"And when you're done with the article in the *Aid* book, you must read First and Second Samuel out of this Bible; it's also all about what people thought—and still think—of you."

"I shall give it my thoughtful attention," David promised.

# 7
## *(October 7, 2001) (One month later)*

After having closely monitored the poisoned David for several hours in the emergency room, they had transferred him to a semi-private room in the ICU. The massive dosage of sodium pentobarbital they had finally decided to give him seemed to be having a gradual effect for the better.

Now he lay prone, with oxygen tubes strapped to his nose. Peter sat on a chair beside the bed, watching David's monitored heartbeat as if hypnotized.

"How's he doing?"

The voice startled Peter and he turned to see Jonathan Ingles standing at the foot of the bed, a concerned look on his face.

"It's Jonathan, right? I've heard David talk about you." Peter held out his hand, and Jonathan shook it feebly.

"Listen, Jonathan," Peter said. "David's not doing so well. They want to give him a blood transfusion, so we need to sneak him out of here."

Jonathan looked doubtful. "After hearing his talk, are you sure he'd be against a transfusion?"

"Maybe not," Peter agreed. He was about to resign himself to the situation; everything had been going so well until David had pushed too far and the Governing Body had decided to get rid of him. Now nothing was going right. Peter hoped David would recover, since he'd gotten him into this mess, but he knew that when he did he'd put it all together and that meant prison for Peter.

"I know why you want him out of here," Jonathan said with a defiant look.

"You do?" Peter asked with more dejection than surprise.

"Yes. But I have my own reasons for helping you. David has become like a father to me, and I worry about them coming in here and trying to finish him off."

"I'm fond of him too," Peter said. "I'm really glad you're going to help me. Here's what I want you to do—"

"I'm sick and tired of taking orders," Jonathan interrupted. "That's one thing David taught me: *I'm* in charge! Besides, you've really botched things up, you know. You've managed by sheer luck to wrest some power over this organization, and instead of pushing through to the conclusion, you've let it get all fouled up. Well, I'm made of sterner stuff: at least now, thanks to my recent education about the Governing Body.

"Maybe you've gotten all you want out of this deal, but now it's *my* turn, and I want much more. I want to see them *crawl*. I want to utterly destroy them.

"I'm going to have to take over this operation from here on in. If you don't like it, I'll just have to have a little talk about you with Detective Kramer. He's already suspicious of you, you know."

Peter stared at Jonathan in dumb surprise.

Seeing that he was at a loss for words, Jonathan took charge: "Here's the plan: you go distract them at the nurses' station while I hook myself up to his monitor."

"How are you going to do that without getting it all fouled up?" Peter asked doubtfully.

"I know how because sister Foley described it to me in minute detail. By the time they check the monitors at their station they'll never know the difference. A moment of interference from the patient turning over or something: they won't bother to check.

"Then come back in here and we'll put David in his absent roommate's wheelchair, and you can wheel him out of here, if you're careful. I've got my blood brother waiting in a car across the street. I'll wait fifteen minutes after you're gone, and then I'll sneak out of here too. Then we're going to drive him to a clinic my dad runs in Defiance, Ohio. He'll admit him as a John Doe.

"No one will know if he made it or died: we'll be able to play it whichever way works best to our advantage. If the Governing Body announces that Jehovah destroyed him (which I'm pretty sure they will), we can threaten to produce him in order to embarrass them. Or we can just keep quiet and let them take a murder rap.

"Now help me hook myself up to the monitor cables they took off of his roommate, then I'll be able to unplug David's cables from the hub and plug in mine in less than a second while you're at the nurses' station distracting them."

# Layer Five

**1**
*(September 3, 2001) (One month earlier)*

Jonathan lay in his bed, in the middle of the floor, surrounded by the beds of his roommates: Tony and Jim, on either side. None of them slept.

"What did you think of tonight's *Watchman* study?" Tony asked.

"Same old, same old," Jim replied with a sigh.

"Hey, don't discourage the newbie," Tony laughed.

"Maybe the newbie is already discouraged," Jonathan said. "Maybe I was discouraged before I ever came to Bethel."

"Were you brought up in the truth, like us?" Tony asked.

"Yeah," Jonathan replied.

"I can always tell," Jim said. "We've got one young brother at our table, and he just never shuts up about the truth all through breakfast. Been in the truth a little over a year."

"Only a year! I'm surprised they let him in," Tony remarked.

"I don't think they *let* him in," Jim laughed, "I think he pounded on the door till they *gave* in!"

They all laughed over this, and then Jonathan said in a more serious vein: "Do you ever wish it weren't the truth? You know what I mean?"

"Yeah," they both answered.

"It's like sure, we've got the truth and the New Order will be great and all that, but it sure messes up our lives here and now."

"Like not playing football," Tony lamented.

"Or going to college," Jonathan said.

"Or dating interesting chicks," Jim laughed.

"That's sort of why I'm here," Jonathan told them.

"What?" Jim cried, "I hate to break the news, brother, but you ain't gonna meet any women here at Bethel!'"

When Tony and Jim finished laughing, Jonathan explained himself. "What I mean is I'm here on account of a woman."

"Ah, our new roommate has a past!" Andy remarked.

"Now you've got to tell your roommates all about it," Jim declared.

"Well, you see, I met this woman out in field service—"

"Not a *householder!*" Jim cried, "Oh man! That's too much!"

"Yes, a householder," Jonathan replied. "She was the most beautiful woman I'd ever seen. I gave her a witness, and she invited me back. And, we quickly fell for each other. The only thing is: I was on vacation at the time: visiting out of state. When I had to go back home, she begged me to stay, but I couldn't."

"Of course not; she being in the world," Tony said.

"I would've stayed with her anyway, but for my father. When I told him about it he went ballistic. He would've disowned me, and I would've lost everything. He's got a thriving clinic in Defiance, Ohio, and that's my inheritance. So, he made me come here to Bethel to forget about her and be "upbuilded" by associating with guys like you."

They all laughed at this.

"But even if it weren't for my father," Jonathan concluded, "you can't just leave the truth. Give up an eternity of perfect happiness in the New World for a few years of happiness in this old world? That would just be stupid."

"You're right, brother," both his roommates agreed, and drifted off to sleep.

But Jonathan lay awake for a good hour tormenting himself with how he'd sacrificed love for truth.

**2**
*(September 16, 2001) (Two weeks later)*

David and Jonathan walked into the local precinct. They were quickly directed to Detective Kramer's office.

"So, you're David Jesseson and Jonathan Ingles," Detective Kramer said, "any proof of that?"

"I have my Ohio driver's license," Jonathan said, pulling it out of his wallet.

Detective Kramer looked at it briefly, comparing the photo to the face before him, then holding it up to the light in order to spot any fakery. Seemingly satisfied with its genuineness, he handed it back and turned to David. "What about you?" he asked.

"I'm afraid I am without ID," David said.

"You know your Social Security Number?"

"Yes."

Detective Kramer typed something on his notebook computer, then turned it around to face David. "Type in the numbers and press Enter; we've got a new policy protecting Social Security Numbers from even *our* eyes unless absolutely necessary, so this saves me a lot of paperwork if you'll type it in yourself.

David typed in some numbers and hit Enter, then turned the notebook back towards Detective Kramer, who studied it for a while, typing some more, reading some more... until the bemused look on his face changed to an amused one.

"Can you tell me, Mr. Jesseson, whether you were being held against your will by anyone at anytime?" he asked.

"We were, briefly. We wanted to take a walk, and were physically prevented from doing so. Of course, in my younger days, such ruffians would not have prevailed. But I thought it the better part of valor to wait until the men had both nodded off and then walk out quietly, together with my friend, Jonathan."

"Would either of you like to press charges against the men who held you?"

"Certainly not," Jonathan said indignantly. "They are our brothers. They were just obeying orders."

"Orders from whom?"

"I'd rather not say."

"Very well, gentlemen." He said, picking up the phone. "Sergeant? Let Bruce Kline and Henry Henderson go; the men they supposedly kidnapped are sitting in my office, and they're not pressing charges. Okay? Thanks."

"Thanks for coming in, gentlemen," he told David and Jonathan. "You may go."

The two nodded to him and walked to the door.

"Uh, Mr. Jesseson," Detective Kramer called out as they reached the door, "I'd like to talk to you alone for a moment."

Jonathan walked out the door and shut it discreetly behind him.

David resumed his seat.

Detective Kramer stared at him for a few moments and then asked, "What sort of a game are you playing, Mr. Jesseson?"

"Game?"

"Yes, you may fool these fundamentalists into thinking you're King David back from the dead, but you don't fool me. I'm not a Bible scholar, but I'd venture to guess that very few people in Biblical times had a Social Security Number. I have your birth information right up here on the screen, and the date is not B.C.E. Should I read it to you? What sort of a con are you up to?"

"I am what is needed," David replied softly, with a far away look on his face. "Miracles are provided as needed: even miracles of information."

"And the oblique allusion you made to 'discretion is the better part of valor'?" Detective Kramer asked. "We detectives aren't totally without culture: I know that's fifteenth century Shakespeare.

"It says here on my screen that your ex-wife has filed a missing-person's report on you. Did you know that?"

"I have eleven wives," David said, "I can't keep track of them all and let them know my whereabouts every moment. Let's see, there's Michal," he began counting them off on his fingers, "Ahinoam, Abigail, Maacah, Haggith, Abital, Eglah, Bath-sheba..."

"A bigamist to boot, huh? Well, Ann Carter is the *ex*-wife who filed the report, ring any bells?"

"Ann? Ann Carter?" David repeated the name as if remembering something long forgotten.

"Would you like to talk to her? She left a contact number. It would help me close out the file if you would."

"Talk to her?" he asked, turning pale.

"Yes, won't take but a moment," Detective Kramer promised as he dialed the phone.

"Ann. Ann Carter," David repeated to himself again, seemingly without much comprehension. The next thing he knew a phone was placed next to his ear and a tiny voice was speaking to him.

"Dad? Dad, it's Sarah. Where the hell are you? Mom is frantic; she's filed a missing persons report on you. Tell me you haven't gone off as Socrates again somewhere. Dad? Dad, are you listening to me?"

David looked up with a puzzled expression. "That's my daughter," he said.

"Evidently. How does a man from umpteen B.C.E. come to have a young daughter in 2001 C.E.?"

"It's not possible," David admitted. "I've been taken for a ride."

"*You* have?"

"Yes. I must tell Jonathan that he was right: I'm David, but not the David they told me I was."

"Someone *told* you that you were King David?"

"They'll all be so disappointed," David said sadly.

Detective Kramer spoke briefly to Sarah, letting her know her father was all right. After he hung up he told David: "Wait here, please."

He stepped out of the office and told a waiting Jonathan: "This man is not King David. I don't think he knows *who* he is. I'm sending him over to Bellevue for evaluation."

"How do you know?" Jonathan asked.

"He's got a family out in California looking for him."

"I see," Jonathan said, looking more disappointed than surprised.

"You'd better head back to your people on your own, son."

Jonathan stood up and walked slowly out of the precinct without looking back.

When Detective Kramer walked back into his office, David looked up at him and said, "There is someone that I *would* like to press charges against."

"Yes, and who might that be?"

"Peter Frawley, the journalist."

"On what charge?"

"Kidnapping."

But after David related the details of the crime, Detective Kramer dismissed it as more fantasy of the deluded man.

"Well, that happened in California," he told him by way of excuse, "this is New York: I'm afraid it's out of my jurisdiction. You'll have to contact the authorities in San Diego if you want to pursue it."

The intercom on his desk buzzed and he was informed that Henderson and Kline wanted to come in and see David immediately.

"Send them in," he said.

"David!" Bruce exclaimed as he and Henderson rushed into the room.

"You can't imagine how glad we are to see you," Henderson remarked dryly.

"Are you done with him, and can we all go now?" Bruce asked.

"Well," Detective Kramer said, "I don't know. This man seems very confused about who he is. I was going to transfer him to Bellevue for observation."

"Listen," Henderson said with a warning tone in his voice, "it is our religious belief that this man is King David. We don't expect you to understand that, but we expect you to respect our religious belief and not violate our freedom of religion."

"Very well," Detective Kramer agreed, glad to be free of the paperwork, "I'll release him into your custody.

**3**

That evening, David and Jonathan were back in their room as usual. They sat on the bed staring out the window: thinking but not talking. But after about an hour of this, David broke the silence.

"You were right, Jonathan: I'm not King David."

"I know, Detective Kramer told me."

"I'm sorry. I was confused. You see, I have this personality disorder where I try to be who I think people want me to be."

"Well, I guess everyone suffers from that to some degree." Jonathan said. "And we all sure wanted you to be David!"

"Yes, but I didn't do it deliberately. You see, I was abducted. And when I was hit on the head I think I forgot who I was even more than usual. And then that Peter Frawley took advantage of the situation and convinced me that I was King David.

"I don't know how to break the news to the others. It took me this long to figure out how to tell you, and I'm closer to you than to any of them."

Jonathan thought this over for a while, and then he asked, "What if we don't tell them right away?"

"But that would be dishonest."

"Maybe, but really we'll just let them think what they've already convinced themselves of, and maybe some greater good could come from it."

"How so?"

"You remember sister Foley?"

"Of course; I shall never forget that dear woman and her tragic death."

"We have a chance, you and I, to prevent such tragedies from ever occurring again."

"But they wouldn't listen to me when I told them what I thought about that."

"You went to the Governing Body," Jonathan explained. "Of course *they're* not going to listen; they think they're the exclusive pipeline to God himself! You need a chance to address the average Watchman, and it's only in the guise of King David that they'll ever listen to you over the Governing Body. Let's just bide our time until that opportunity presents itself."

They fell silent for several minutes: idly watching the men across the street milling about the entrance of the Hotel Margaret.

Then Jonathan chuckled.

"What?" David asked.

"I was just thinking how improbable this all is: you and I sitting here at Bethel: you a professor, having been abducted and led to believe you were King David as a means to someone else's ends; and my now using that odd occurrence to—uh—avenge the death of sister Foley and all those like her. It almost seems beyond the laws of chance: like Jehovah was guiding it all."

"Ah, yes," David remarked, "the gods! Socrates didn't believe in them you know. He thought it ludicrous to think of the gods as having desires, and human-like jealousies and machinations. He thought it was obvious that they were just projections of people's own feelings and thoughts. I'm sure he would've said the same thing about your Jehovah."

"But how do you explain creation without a Creator?" Jonathan asked. "The odds of life arising spontaneously are trillions to one!"

"Well, as you pointed out," David replied, "the odds against you and I sharing this room in these circumstances and having this conversation are also astronomical. Yet it is happening.

"The odds against *any* particular set of circumstances occurring is always mind boggling. Yet, *something* will always happen. You and I must be somewhere right now, and it is equally improbable that we would be in any particular place talking with any particular person out of the billions of people and places in the world. Yet, the odds that we will be *somewhere* doing *something* are one in one."

"I'm not sure I follow the relevance of that," Jonathan admitted.

"Shoot an arrow straight up into the air on a day with gusty, variable winds," David said. "Who can say precisely where it will land? Or flip a coin: who can predict with certainty whether it will come up heads or tails?"

"No one," Jonathan replied.

"But, who would be so foolish to conclude from that fact that the arrow will not land in any particular place, or that the coin will not come up heads *or* tails?"

"No one, again," Jonathan said.

"You see: the odds against our lives playing out exactly as they have are like billions of flips of that coin all coming up certain ways. Countless events have shaped our personalities and circumstances. Few if any could've been predicted. But in every case something would've happened, and our personalities would be molded and our circumstances changed. If we were to look back now on our lives as events that were leading us to this moment we would conclude that our lives are impossibly improbable.

"But, if we look at it aright, we see that our lives, at every moment, had a one-to-one chance of transpiring as they did (since something had to happen, and what happened was just as likely as any other happenstance).

"Our lives were not somehow consciously leading up to this point (if they had been, then yes, that would be astronomically improbable) they were just meandering along—and this is where we've come to.

"So too, with what you call 'creation': if we think of it as having purposely tried to reach this particular blend of species on the planet with all of their interrelated ecosystems, we'd conclude that it is highly improbable. But when we realize that interactions would naturally occur, and that *something* would eventually result, we realize that it's not improbable at all. It's equally probable that other life forms could've evolved, and life could be far different from what we experience today, but that scenario had an equal chance with the one we see before us today.

"To go back to the analogy of the arrow: let's say that after it lands we circle the spot. That's equivalent to biologists classifying the species we have today. But Creationists look at that circle and imagine that it could've somehow been made before the arrow landed; that someone *intended* it to land just there, and they cry: Impossible! And, of course, they're right; that would've been impossible, but they're not looking at it aright. The circle is drawn afterwards: the complexity is recognized only after it has evolved over millions of years.

"What seems impossible to *me* is to think that out of all of the interactions over billions of years between atoms, and eventually molecules—that *nothing* would've happened: that life *wouldn't* have evolved. Even at the atomic level there are atoms which have needs that other atoms can meet."

Jonathan laughed at this. "Atoms with needs?"

"I'm serious," David said. "Atoms lacking their balanced number of electrons need to acquire an electron, just as atoms with too many electrons need to shed them. These unbalanced atoms attract one another and exchange electrons to achieve stasis. In some cases they bond together.

"The same thing happens on the macro level, where we call such bonding *friendship*, or at the highest level: *love*."

"Okay, but who created those atoms?" Jonathan asked.

"No one," David replied.

"How can you believe that something was created without a creator?" Jonathan asked.

"But you believe that your 'creator' was created without a creator," David pointed out. "It seems infinitely more improbable to me that a full-blown omnipotent, intelligent being would've sprung into existence out of nothing than that mindless atoms exploded and gradually interacted to form what we see today."

At this, David rolled over in his bed, assumed the fetal position, and said, "Good night." He was snoring loudly and happily within two minutes.

When Jonathan was sure that David was dead to the world, he quietly walked out of the room, and made his way to brother Kline's room.

He knocked softly on the door, and when it opened he told a bewildered Bruce: "Time for my nightly report."

"Yes, of course," Bruce replied, stepping aside to allow him into the room.

"Where tonight?" Jonathan asked, removing his robe.

Bruce stared back in puzzlement.

"Where do you want to do it?" Jonathan clarified. "On the bed, or standing, like we did in the shower the first time we met?"

"Make your report first," Bruce ordered sternly. "Then I'll decide if you deserve it."

Jonathan appeared to give this some thought, then said: "There's nothing to report. He's been behaving himself since we got back."

"Why did you allow him to leave in the first place?" Bruce demanded. "You cost us a great deal of trouble, young man!"

"I wasn't about to say No to King David!"

"Well, report to me immediately if he gets up to something like that again. We can't afford to have him running around like a loose canon! Now bend over the bed."

Jonathan slowly walked over to the bed, pulled down his pajama bottoms, and placed his head and upper body gently on the soft bedspread.

"You were a bad boy and you must be punished," Bruce said, taking a switch and a bottle of baby oil from his bureau drawer.

As he lay there, wincing in pain and disgust, Jonathan promised himself that someday he would have some sort of power or something to hold over this man, and the situation would be reversed. As he told David: he just had to bide his time.

# Layer Six

**1**
*(October 15, 2001) (One month later)*

Peter had been back in San Diego for three days and he still hadn't heard from Mary. In desperation he paid a visit to the house: hoping against all logic that she would somehow be there.

A young man in a three-piece suit answered the door, a *Watchman* magazine and yellow highlighter in one hand. "Yes," he said in a suspicious tone, "can I help you?"

"My fiancé used to live here," Peter explained with a smile.

"They moved out," the young man replied curtly. "We're the new owners now."

"Did the former owners leave a forwarding address?"

"No."

"Mind if I ask you a question?" Peter said, sensing a possible story.

"What?"

"Well, obviously you've been posted here by the Watchmen to welcome back the next 'Ancient Worthy' that appears on this doorstep. So, who are you expecting next?"

"Oh, probably Abraham or Jacob," the young man replied with a nervous smile. "Are you a brother?"

"I used to be—until the organization started killing people who disagreed with them."

The young man appeared stunned at this comment, and availed himself of a privilege often practiced upon the Watchmen but seldom performed by them: he slammed the door in Peter's face—with great satisfaction.

That slamming door made for a good ending to Peter's series of articles on David and the Watchmen. The following day, after dropping off the articles at the *San Diego Reader*, he decided to contact the one person he was sure would know of Mary's whereabouts.

It was Ramsees Mason who answered Peter's knock on the dorm door.

"What you want, man?"

"I want to talk to your boss."

"My *boss*?"

"You know: the guy who calls himself Laurel."

"I don't know no Laurel," he said, and slammed the door.

It was opened a second later by Joel Grey, who grabbed Peter's shirt in his large fist and yanked him into the room.

"You're either stupid or you got brass balls comin' here."

Peter looked him calmly in the eye and said, "The last time I spoke with your boss it turned out very profitable for him. Now I have a new deal with even higher stakes. I'd hate to be you two when he finds out you kept me away from him."

"Get rid of him, man!" Ramsees pleaded.

"No, no," Joel said, "what's the harm? We'll give the man what he wants, and if it don't pan out, Mr. L. will have us kick his butt. Either way, there's money in it for us."

They drove him out to Pacific Heights, to a magnificent mansion with an ocean view.

They kept Peter between them as they walked up to the house: it reminded him of how they had escorted David from the college campus just six weeks ago. But Peter had paid Mary's debt in full, so he knew he had nothing to fear from 'Mr. L'.

They rang the doorbell, and waited. Finally an intercom voice, distorted almost past recognition by excessive volume, asked, "Can I help you?"

"Mason and Grey to see Mr. L," Ramsees yelled into the intercom.

"You have to push the button first, idiot," Joel told him with exaggerated exasperation.

But before Ramsees could push the button, the door swung open. A short woman in a maid's outfit stood to one side and motioned them in. "They're in the parlor," she informed them as she walked back into the kitchen without bothering to look at them.

"C'mon," Joel said, tugging on Peter's sleeve. But Peter was frozen in place. He could hear the sound of a piano coming from down the hall. It was Chopin's *"Heroic" Polonaise*: the music Mary had played for him so many times.

"C'mon, man," Ramsees said, and together the two men pulled him down the hall and into the parlor.

Mr. L. was sitting on an overstuffed leather recliner. He was in a dressing gown, smoking a pipe, and evidently enjoying the music.

A grand piano stood on the far wall. With its back facing the room, its player was hidden from view behind the music stand. Peter thought that the piano looked just like Mary's.

Mr. L. looked up and put a finger to his lips, indicating that silence should be observed. Then he closed his eyes and leaned his head back: a smile of pure pleasure on his face.

When the final note had been played he said, "That was lovely, my dear. Now come out from behind your piano; we have company."

Peter watched in shock as Mary emerged from behind the piano. She started to smile when she saw him, but then quickly looked down at her feet, stopping dead in her tracks, her face flushed.

"Have a seat," Mr. L. said with a nod to Joel and Ramsees who dumped Peter onto the leather couch.

"What brings you here?" Mr. L. asked, relighting his pipe.

Ignoring him, Peter addressed Mary: "Mary, where have you been? You stopped returning my calls. I've been back in town for days looking for you."

"She's been here, with me," Mr. L. said. Then he took a puff of his pipe, and blew a small smoke-ring.

"With *you*?" Peter said in shock. "Look, we've paid you all we owe you, now let her go!"

"I'm afraid it's not that simple," Mr. L. said. "Why don't you explain it to him, dear?"

"You're cruel," she said accusingly. Then she stormed out of the room.

"You see," Mr. L. explained, "Mary and I are married. Have been for about a year and a half.

"Oh, we've had our ups and downs, Mary and me: mostly financial troubles, you know. We really were in some serious debt to some really serious dudes. Guys who make me look like Prince Charming.

"It was Mary who came up with the idea originally. 'Honey,' she said—that's what she calls me: *Honey*. Did she make up any pet names for you?"

Peter just stared at him, trying to take it all in.

"Well, it doesn't matter. None of my business what you two did; that's in the past, and I'm willing to let bygones be bygones: which is what you'll do too if you're smart.

"Anyway, 'Honey,' she says to me, 'if a man is desperately in love, he'll do anything to protect his lover. *Anything*: even if it isn't strictly legal or moral: even if the man is usually a law-abiding, moral person.'

"When you stumbled into our lives, we knew immediately that you were the right type: a love-sick puppy. We knew you'd come up with some scheme to rescue the maiden in distress, and that you'd take most of the risk. So, we've stayed out of your way this whole time, just playing out the part you assigned us: negotiating for the maximum amount we could get out of the Watchmen for that white elephant her dad had left her."

He put his pipe down and stood up, yawning and stretching. "But now you've served your purpose. It's time for us all to get on with our separate lives. I'm afraid you must forget about Mary and me. Or else we'll arrange it so that you'll be in no position to ever remember anything ever again."

"Boys," he said, as he turned to leave the room, "show him out with the usual send-off so he won't forget how rough we play."

"No," Mary cried, running back into the room. "Leave him alone. Haven't we hurt him enough already?"

Mr. L. turned back to look at her. He stared at her for a long while. At first he was angry that she would contradict him, but slowly, almost imperceptibly, he began to grin and shake his head. "Well, well, well: it looks as though someone got involved here. Very unprofessional, my dear. But, as I've always said: I'm a generous man. If you want to keep him as a plaything, I won't stand in your way. I have several playthings of my own—like Jenny— as I'm sure you're painfully aware. Just remember who owns you at the end of the day.

"Let him go boys," he said, "they're both just lovesick fools: too wrapped up in their own illusions to pose us any threat." and he walked out of the room.

"What a waste of time!" Mason said, and he and Grey walked out the front door.

Mary and Peter stood alone in the room staring at each other.

"Oh, I hate him so!" Mary exclaimed. "And that's a damn lie about Jenny. He just said that to hurt me." Then she looked down at her feet again, and whispered: "I'm sorry, Peter. Truly."

Peter turned around and slowly walked out of the house.

# Layer Seven

**1**

*(January 12, 2002) (Three months later)*

"My next guest is the author of the current best-seller: *Socrates Atop the Watchtower: How one emotionally-challenged man's truth toppled a religious empire*. The author is Jon Ingles, he's a former member of what he now acknowledges is a religious cult, and this is his first foray into the world of publishing, so let's give him a warm welcome."

The sound of applause emerged from Mary's bedroom television just as her husband walked into the room.

"What sort of crap are you watching now?" he asked.

"Quiet!" she said with a dismissive gesture. "This is something that might interest you, Harry."

"Oh, really?" he said doubtfully as he sat down on the edge of her bed.

On the TV program Jonathan had also taken his seat: next to the talk-show host who was already asking his first question.

"In your book you describe a man with a personality disorder similar to Woody Allen's *Zelig*: a chameleon man who assumed the characteristics of those around him. Can you tell us what it was like being around such a man?"

"David was like a father figure to me," Jonathan said. "He was a very kind and thoughtful man."

"But he did have this personality disorder," the host interrupted.

"Well, yes, but I'd hate to have him be remembered just for that. He was a professor of philosophy—"

"He thought he was King David, back from the dead, did he not?" the host asked, trying to prod Jonathan into saying something entertaining.

"At one point he did," Jonathan admitted.

"And this religious group you were with at that time: the 'Watchmen', they believed it too, didn't they?"

"Yes, we were all convinced."

"And didn't I read at one point that they held him hostage, and then finally murdered him?"

"Yes, you see David was an original thinker and he spoke out against the cult's prohibition on blood transfusions."

"Ah yes," the host interjected. "These are the people who refuse blood transfusions, aren't they?"

"Yes."

"Tell me, Jonathan, when you were a Watchman, would you have allowed your child to have a blood transfusion if their life depended on it?"

"I don't have any children."

"But if you did?"

"No, I wouldn't have allowed it. But David convinced me— and most of the other Watchmen—that their stance on blood was wrong."

"And is that why you left?"

"Not just that. It was a very abusive atmosphere. Those with the power in the organization aren't hesitant to wield it to *run*—and *ruin* people's lives."

"But tell me more about the kidnapping and murder," the host urged, almost salivating.

"David was giving a talk in which he stated that it is our *duty* to donate blood, and that's when they poisoned him."

"And you saw them do that?"

"Yes."

"Did anyone else see it?"

"There were several thousand witnesses. That's why one of their leaders: Melvin Hershey is sitting in prison for attempted murder."

"*Attempted* murder?"

"Yes, you need a body to prove murder, and the body disappeared."

"What about the kidnapping, Jon?"

"That wasn't done by the Watchmen. It was a journalist by the name of Peter Frawley."

"Damn!" Harry shouted, physically shaking the bed.

"What?" Mary asked, more annoyed at the outburst than curious.

"If they connect your Peter with the kidnapping, they'll trace it back to us."

"How do you figure that?"

"They'll question him about his involvement, and he'll blab about us."

"Why would he do that?"

"Oh, you're so stupid!" Harry yelled in scorn. "Sure, the lovesick puppy would do anything to rescue you, but now he's been spurned. So now he'll do anything for revenge."

"Peter's not like that." Mary said, and then whispered, "He's not like *you*."

"Well, I'll just have the boys pay him another little visit and put the fear of me back into him."

Mary gave the back of his head a hateful look, then returned her attention to the TV.

Jonathan was saying, "The few Watchmen who still haven't left the cult claim that David was 'destroyed' by God for speaking against their organization. That's why they say the body disappeared: God obliterated all traces of it."

"That's a pretty incredible thing to believe," the host noted.

"Yes, but for them it's preferable to thinking that their leaders could've made a mistake, or committed a crime.

"But I'm happy to report that David didn't die. He has been recuperating in my father's clinic ever since the poisoning. He's here today, making his first public appearance since the attack."

"Well, let's bring him on out!" the host exclaimed. "Ladies and gentlemen, the man who toppled a religious empire: David Jesseson!"

David emerged from behind the curtain. Supported on the arm of his daughter Sarah, he walked slowly over to Jonathan and embraced him.

Harry turned to look at Mary. His face wore a shocked and worried expression. "That bastard can identify Mason and Grey!"

"No great loss there," Mary commented.

"You're so damn stupid! They'll squeal on me the first chance they get!"

Mary couldn't help taunting him: "What is that they say about 'if you can't do the time, don't do the crime?'"

"Listen, bitch!" Harry screamed, moving around the bed, "If I go down, you go down!" He struck her across the face with his fist and yelled: "This whole thing was your damned idea!"

She buried her face in the pillow, sobbing.

"Listen!" he yelled, pulling her head out of the pillow by her hair. "I want you to hear this so you'll stay as deeply involved as me. I'm gonna have to take out both Peter Frawley and this David Jesseson. And don't give me any shit about it because we both know it's all your fault. I'm not going down for this. But I promise you that if I do, I won't go down alone!"

Harry left, and Mary lay sobbing for a while, thinking about how much she hated him, and how guilty she felt about having hurt Peter.

On the TV program a new guest had sat down between Jonathan and the talk-show host. Mary gathered that he was some sort of politician.

"Do they really have 'weapons of mass destruction'?" the host asked him.

"Of course," he replied, evidently surprised that anyone would question this.

"How do we know this?" David asked.

"Because, President Bush, the most powerful and best informed man on the planet, has told us."

"Assuming that he is, in fact, the best informed man," David said, "I think we must also ask if he is the most *honest* man on the planet. It is said that power corrupts, so does this 'most powerful man' have any motivation to lie to us about this matter?"

"Listen," the politician said, raising his voice. "All of you bleeding-heart liberals should get down on your knees and thank God for President Bush. He's the one who is saving this country from terrorism."

"But isn't it true," David continued, nonplussed, "that this president got into office dishonestly?"

"No, that is *not* true!"

"More people voted for Gore than Bush," the host reminded him.

"Well, in this country it is the electorate that elects the president: not the popular vote. I think you just need to learn a little more about how your government works."

"Isn't it also true," David said, "that this usurper—pardon me, I mean 'president'—" This garnered a few laughs and applause from the studio audience. "Isn't it true that he has a vested interest in oil?"

"He has been in the oil business, that's true," the politician conceded. "There's no law against that."

"And do you think that it's just a coincidence that the places he wants to bomb and take over have the world's richest oil reserves?"

"They are harboring terrorists!" The politician exclaimed. "We must bomb them for our own self-defense!"

"Must we?" David asked. "Let's turn the situation around. Let's say that some radical fringe group from *our* country—like the Ku Klux Klan, for instance—went over to *their* country and blew up a building, and then came back to the U.S. and hid out somewhere where law enforcement was unable to find them. Would you then say that the other country was justified in dropping bombs on the U.S. for 'harboring terrorists'?"

The politician seemed unsure of how to answer this, so David turned to the host and asked: "Do you think they would be justified in declaring war on the entire United States, and unashamedly announcing their intention to kill innocent civilians?"

"Well, no," the host replied hesitantly.

"Of course not," David agreed. "You don't punish an entire country for the actions of a few criminals within it. But that is what Bush has done. And I, for one, am not about to 'thank God' for his crimes against humanity."

"It's just like how we refused to be ruled by the Governing Body of the Watchmen when we found out that they were wrong." Jonathan said. "What David has taught me is that it's vital that we think for ourselves and not just accept as true whatever our leaders tell us. They really only have power over us when we *give* them that power, and that means that ultimately *we* are in charge."

"No," the politician said, "we are *not* in charge; that's anarchy. That's why we set up a government to rule us. They know what's best, and if they make mistakes sometimes, we just have to agree to live with that, because it's better than anarchy."

"But, don't you see," David said, "blindly playing 'following the leader' leads to something much worse than anarchy: a mindless, potentially cruel society."

"Like Nazi Germany," Jonathan added.

"Yes," David agreed. "In Nazi Germany people were being led by a madman, and everyone was afraid to break out of that nightmare because it had become an all-encompassing illusion. Religion and patriotism can lead to the same state when people stop thinking for themselves and just implicitly trust that their leaders can do no wrong."

"Or," Jonathan said, "that *they* themselves can do no wrong as long as they do and think whatever their leaders say."

"I think," David said, "that one must be true to one's nature, and human nature is essentially empathetic. We are happiest when we are doing what we instinctively feel is right. If we make life better for someone else, we have automatically made life better for ourselves: we have achieved nirvana—at least for a while. That feeling far outweighs any religious or patriotic ideal, and it can never lead to the kind of moral outrages and human tragedies that those ideals have visited upon humankind throughout history."

Mary aimed the remote at the TV and hit the power button. The men on the screen quickly shrunk into blackness and silence filled the room. She wiped her eyes on a tissue, and slowly got out of bed.

As she began packing a small suitcase she could hear Harry on the phone in the den: 'get your butts over here' he was telling Mason and Grey. She knew what he was going to tell them when they got there. She also knew now what she had to do.

**2**
*(March 15, 2002) (Two months later)*

Peter cautiously approached the Caucasian section of the prison yard. His eyes met those of the only person he recognized: Melvin Hershey.

"I'll let you sit here," Hershey told him, "only because I know you'd get killed in any other section. But don't think I'm going to associate with you. I heard what you did, and the Bible warns us against associating with murderers."

"And what are *you*, if not a murderer?" Peter asked.

"That was an execution of God's will," Hershey explained. "It's not 'murder' to carry out God's will. Rather, it's a service. In warfare soldiers are not murderers: they are '*service* men'. I have served God in theocratic warfare, and I have sacrificed my own freedom for Jehovah."

"So you see yourself as noble?" Peter asked.

"You wouldn't understand," Hershey said. "You're just a common criminal: who murdered his rival in a sordid love triangle."

"If you were acting on God's will," Peter said, "how come David is still alive? Is God's will so easily thwarted? It would seem your sacrifice was for nothing."

"He's *not* still alive," Hershey replied defensively. "Jehovah destroyed him. I was just the instrument that he used to end his life. But Jehovah himself disintegrated the body."

"The truth is," Peter said, "not only did David survive, but he's been on TV for all the world to see."

Hershey shook his head as if out of pity for Peter's stupidity. "That's an imposter," he said, "someone who has been demon-possessed and made to look like David. The real David has gone into the second death and will never be seen again. Just like what's going to happen to you.

"But as for me," Hershey said, as he stood to go. "I think I'll be out of here pretty soon now that the world thinks that David didn't die. It's like everything else that happens in the world: Jehovah eventually uses it to work good for his name people. Too bad for you that you're no longer one of us; you'll rot in here."

"It's ironic," Peter said, though Hershey had already begun walking away. "You think *you're* innocent and that *I'm* guilty, when the truth is just the opposite." It felt good to say this, but then he got to thinking and realized that maybe *all* prisoner's thought they were innocent while everyone else was guilty. Maybe that was the situation outside of prison as well.

"Frawley," the guard said, "you've got a visitor."

They ushered Peter out of the yard, through countless hallways and gates, until he came to the visiting room. He sat down on his side of the heavy glass and picked up the phone.

"Hi," Mary said. "How are you?"

"I'm fine," Peter replied, failing at his attempt to sound convincing.

It was the first time they had seen each other since her husband's murder and Peter's subsequent arrest.

"Peter, why did you confess?"

"I knew I could bear it in here better than you. Not that I'm stronger, but you're too full of life to survive cooped up like this."

"But you didn't do it!"

"Look," he said softly, "when I heard he'd been shot, I knew it had to have been you protecting me from him. I figured he'd come after me eventually; I was his loose end. And after Jonathan and David appeared on TV I knew he'd be coming soon.

"You saved my life by taking his. I couldn't sit back and watch you go to prison for that. Confessing to the crime was the least I could do."

"I love you," she said. "I'm so sorry I let Harry use you."

"Don't love me anymore," Peter said with a sigh; "I couldn't bear that either. You need to find someone out there who's free." He turned his head away and added, "Consider me dead."

"But how could I abandon you now?" Mary asked, her chin starting to quiver. "How could you survive all alone without love?"

"I've done it all my life," Peter said, smiling weakly. "It's enough that there was a brief moment when there was *you*, and there was true love: proven by sacrifices. That will sustain me for the rest of my life. No matter how bad things may get in here, I'll always remember that there was you, and that you loved me."

"A murderess?" Mary asked sadly.

"Time's up!" the guard announced.

"Not a murderess," Peter said; "a *savior*. Don't leave your heart here, and don't come back; this is one of those 'no deposit, no return deals." Then he slowly put down the phone, and gave her a tearful smile. She sat there crying as she watched the guard escort him out of the room.

## Epilogue

Bruce Kline rolled out of bed and stumbled to the window. Although it was a cold, rainy, New York spring day, the room was stifling. He slid open the window for a breath of cool fresh air.

"Hey, I'm trying to sleep!" Herb complained. "Come back to bed. Nobody in the entire St. Margaret gets up this damn early!"

Bruce sighed deeply as he looked across the street at what had once been Bethel. He could hear worldly music blaring from several of the rooms. Then his eyes rested on the new sign on the front of the building:

```
Apostasy Arms Condominiums
-- The Lifestyle of Freedom --
```

"Come keep me warm," Herb pleaded.

Bruce shut the window and pulled the blinds tight shut. He stumbled back into bed and snuggled up to Herb, trying to forget.

# Bonus Layer

# 1

The early afternoon sun was warm without being too hot, the breeze was gentle, and the sound of the ocean was just a soft murmur. Most of the sunbathers were already fast asleep.

Mary watched the children playing in the sand as she rubbed a little more sun-block on her bare legs.

A little girl was performing occasionally successful somersaults in a big circle around her slightly older brother who was sitting in the sand frowning, with arms crossed.

"I'm the sun circling the Earth. You're the Earth." She merrily told him.

"The sun doesn't circle the Earth," he told her sternly. "You're stupid."

"I am the Sun, you are the Earth—play me!" she sang out. Mary smiled, delighted at the child's clever adaptation of Neil Diamond.

The little boy scoffed and shook his head, "Stupid! Stupid! Stupid!" he yelled in exasperation.

The little girl continued her play, happily disregarding him

Mary thought she was the most adorable little girl she'd ever seen: a round little body verging on plump, with short jet-black hair and deep, dark eyes. Mary felt compelled to defend her, and found herself singing a new verse to them: "She is the Sun, you are the Earth. She spins for fun, while you have no mirth."

The children stared at her with puzzled looks, and then ran back to their parents to tell them the astonishing fact that an unknown woman had entered their world and sang to them.

As Mary watched them run across the sand, Jonathan slowly eased himself into the plastic chair next to her, being careful not to spill the strawberry margaritas he had just brought from the bar.

"Hey," he said, "wake up and take your drink."

Mary opened her eyes and took her glass from him silently. She took a sip, and then sighed. "How long was I asleep?"

"Probably since I left: twenty minutes maybe." A beach ball landed beside his chair and he kicked it away. "Lots of kids out today," he observed, as he started applying sun-block to his chest.

She was silent for another minute, and then asked him softly: "Does it ever bother you?"

"What?"

"What we did."

Now it was his turn to be silent. He wasn't sure how to answer this; they hadn't spoken of it until now, and he had assumed—and hoped—she would never broach the subject.

After a few minutes of meditating on the rhythmic ocean waves, he had formulated his answer. "I think of it like this: we brought happiness to all concerned. So, we have nothing to feel guilty about."

"Two men are in prison," she reminded him. "One is dead, and another nearly died and may never be the same."

"That's just the surface," he explained. "You've got to dig deeper."

"Isn't that just a convenient rationalization?" she asked.

"Not at all. Look at Hershey and Frawley sitting in prison. Both of them feel that they're suffering for a noble cause: Hershey as *Jehovah's* slave, and Frawley as *yours*."

She winced at this last remark, and took another sip of her drink.

"Then look at Jesseson," he continued. "He's on top of the world: reconciled with his wife and daughter, doing the talk-show circuit— "

"What about my Harry?" she asked. "You can't say he's happier."

"But he was an evil that we rid the world of!" He told her, astonished that he needed to. "He was hate and selfishness personified, standing in the way of our love. I knew that the first time I saw you: when I called on your house in the door-to-door ministry, and we fell in love at first sight—almost two years ago now."

Mentioning their love, and their long time together, he hoped would snap her out of her current attitude. He was soon lost in his own recollections of how quickly they had fallen for each other, and how he had so eagerly embraced their forbidden love: flying in the face of his father's prudish religion. He smiled.

But her attitude didn't change. She removed her sunglasses and stared at him accusingly. "It doesn't bother you that you killed Harry, and that Peter is in prison for it?"

"No," he said, turning away from her.

"And the Watchmen?" she asked,

Frowning, he replied, "Same thing: *the most good for the most people.* And, in fact, that's where we *really* did the *most* good for the *most* people. We led millions out of that dangerous cult, and financially crippled it to such a degree that it can no longer spread its lies effectively.

"And how else was I ever going to get my father off my back about making Bethel a life-long career choice? He never would've approved of you while still believing in all that Watchman crap! And I didn't even *know* it was crap until David opened my eyes."

"Frawley's twin brother died over the blood-transfusion stance, and he himself was molested as a child," she told him. "Did you know that?"

"So, what are you saying?" He asked, becoming suddenly more defensive and leaning forward in his chair. "Revenge is a purer motive than love and justice?"

"Certainly a simpler: more understandable one," she said.

He thought about telling her of his own sexual abuse at the hands of Bruce Kline, but he didn't want her to ever have such a degraded image of him. Besides, she would know that he was partly responsible for manipulating that situation. So, he decided to attack Peter instead: "Look, Frawley was a simpleton! A great thing fell into his lap and he didn't know what to do with it. He missed his opportunity to fully exact his revenge and avenge his brother. All he could see was rescuing the damsel in distress."

"And isn't that what *you've* done?"

"I've done much more than that," he told her proudly, "I also changed the world for the better. When you called me at Bethel and told me about Peter's plan, and that David and he were arriving at Bethel that night, I sprang into action, placing myself in center stage. And when Frawley dropped the ball, I picked it up and ran with it. I immediately saw not only how to pay off your debts, but how to get rid of Harry and the Watchmen to boot!"

"So, you're the noblest of them all," she said in such a way that he couldn't be sure if she was being sarcastic. "Still," she added, "you can't deny that we *used* people—manipulated them like puppets—to get what we wanted."

Jonathan either had no answer for that, or he thought it better not to answer her in her current mood. Either way, they fell silent again.

The family with the children Mary had sung to now passed by with their folding chairs, blankets, and inflated beach toys. They smiled at Mary and she smiled back. The little girl fell behind to stare at her a little longer, and when her mother called her she jumped, waved at Mary, and then ran to her mother. "She's a good girl who make friends easily," her mother said by way of explanation.

"A little selfish, though," her father said, tapping her on the head, but smiling the while, as if selfishness was an attractive vice to have.

Her mother ignored him, and continued addressing Mary: "I hope you don't mind. Are you all staying at the hotel?"

"Yes," Mary told her.

"Maybe we'll see you around," she said with a hopeful smile, and taking her daughter's hand she walked away.

Mary thought: 'She's not selfish; she just needs security. And she can't help it if people just naturally feel compelled to fulfill her desires. That just means she brings out the best in people.'

"Wait!" Mary called to them, "Wait!" More than anything in the world, she desperately wanted to go with them at that moment.

"Mary!" Jonathan shouted, shaking her chair with his foot so he didn't have to bother getting up from his semi-reclining position.

"What?"

"Wake up! You're talking in your sleep again."

"Oh. What did I say?"

"'Wait! Wait!'" he cried, imitating her desperate tone. "Who were you telling to wait, anyway? Frawley?"

"No," she replied. "My mother."

"Your dead mother? Whew! You're not going to go psycho on me now, are you?"

She frowned at him and said, "Dreaming of one's mother is hardly a psychotic episode.

"You know," she said, continuing their previous conversation from where she'd left off, "you think you're so noble, but some would see *us* as—to use your phrase—the 'personification of hate and selfishness.'"

"Well, such people are short-sighted idiots who can't see beneath the surface," he said.

"Oh," she replied, "so this is one of those 'I'm okay: you're okay' deals, isn't it?"

"No deals," he said sternly, "Deals were *Frawley's* weakness. I don't deal; I just live the plain, raw truth of life." And he walked off towards the water without another word.

She watched him wade in up to his chin and float there: a disembodied head, gently lapped by the ocean. Then she muttered to herself: "But who ever sees more than their own surrounding surface?"

Feeling decidedly *ignoble* herself, she gathered up her things, wrapped herself up in her robe, and left. Walking back to the hotel, she muttered an answer to herself: "No one sees beneath their own surface: at least no one who'll ever be happy."

Back in their room, Mary quickly showered and dressed. Then, as she threw her things into a suitcase, she made a phone call.

"Jenny? Hi, it's me. I'm coming home."

"What about *Jonathan*?" Jenny asked in a jealous tone of voice.

"Oh, he's got a good income from the sale of *Socrates Atop the Watchtower*."

"I was surprised by that; I didn't know he was a writer."

"He's *not* really; the book was mostly plagiarized from the drafts of Peter's articles on the Watchmen that were rejected by the *San Diego Reader* after he was arrested. Peter was working on those articles when they were in Defiance together, watching over David's recovery, and Jonathan saved all the drafts he threw out.

"Besides, not only is Jonathan financially secure, he's also happily basking in the glory of his own reflection. He believes he has single-handedly brought the most happiness to the most people."

"Well," Jenny replied, "I guess it's time for you and I to start enjoying *our* happiness, then."

"I'm comin' home, baby!"

"I'll be waiting with champagne and open arms!"

Mary put down the phone and closed her eyes. She took several relaxed, deep breaths as she pictured Jenny, and their life together. Unlike the men she had known, Jenny regarded Mary as *the* most important thing in her world. A contented, warm smile formed on Mary's face, and she felt once again like the little girl somersaulting on the beach.

# Spam Layer

1

From: spammer@conspiracies.net
Date: Today, 3:02 am
Subject: Truth

Do not delete this message! This is not s-p-a-m. This message contains vital information: information known to only a precious few. I'm about to reveal to you a conspiracy so vast and far-reaching that you will be astonished.

This is information that everyone in the world needs to know. That is why I am sending out this email. I know many people will delete it without reading it: that is their loss: don't let it be yours. The sheep and the goats are being separated: distinguished by those who accept and embrace this message, and those who choose to remain in ignorance.

First, I must tell you how I came upon this knowledge.

I was in Egypt, touring the Great Pyramid of Giza. Fascinated by the sheer size of this miracle in stone. Believe me: once you see it you know that primitive ancient men could not have built it without divine help.

When I emerged from the inner chambers, an elderly man who was standing near the entrance handed me a pamphlet entitled: *"The Bible in Stone: The Divine Plan of the Ages Revealed in the Great Pyramid, by Pastor Russell."*

The other tourists tossed the pamphlet away unread, but I read it with great interest. It explained how the measurements of the pyramid's inner chambers and passageways corresponded to the chronology of the Bible, and reveal that Christ returned in 1874, and took kingdom power—after a harvest period of 40 years—in 1914. So: the first great secret you need to know: *the second coming of Christ has already occurred! God's kingdom on earth rules now!*

The Jehovah's Watchmen used to know this; Pastor Russell was their founder. Pastor Russell even chose to be buried under a monument in the shape of the great pyramid, replete with the symbols of Freemasonry. (I have a pamphlet, free for the asking, describing, in the most moving terms, my visit to Pastor Russell's gravesite, and what I learned from the Pastor even in death.) But the Watchmen have ignored all of this: they have repudiated the pyramid, the wisdom of Freemasonry, and the Divine Plan itself. They strayed from the truth and have gone into darkness. Russell was the angel of the Lord (as foretold in Revelation), Rutherford was the second angel, but he fell into the sin of alcoholism and ended his days in darkness.

Even so, God put up with them: even as he did Israel in days of old: they kept backsliding and he would punish them and then forgive them—until they killed his Son: that was the unforgivable sin. So too, the Watchmen have killed the prophet recently sent to them: King David back from the dead. God will not forgive them this latest outrage and turning of their back on him: they are now lost forever.

That is why I founded the group: The Lord's Watchmen. It is for true believers who acknowledge the fact that God's Kingdom rules, and has been doing so ever since 1914, with Christ at the head. Armageddon has already begun (even the Watchmen recognize this fact) and only the Lord's Watchmen will survive.

The Lord's Watchmen carries on the great work begun by Pastor Russell, and continued (for a time) by Rutherford. It is led by the third angel of Revelation, who—true to the humble spirit exemplified by Pastor Russell— makes no claims to greatness, but serves the household of faith humbly to the best of my ability.

If you want to be part of this group, you need to make a testimony of your belief and willingness to follow the Lord and his angel of the present dispensation. God has revealed to me still more secrets of his Divine Plan of the Ages, and he wants me to gather all of the right-hearted ones into his fold, and reveal all to them.

As a member, you will learn the secrets that I have spent a lifetime gathering in my journeys all around the world:

- All the secrets revealed by the Great Pyramid of Giza. (Greatly extending Pastor Russell's work with up-to-date correlations and verifications between world history and the pyramid.)
- The true meaning of Pastor Russell's gravesite and the Freemasonry symbolism found there.
- How it was foretold in the Bible that Rutherford would fall away and would be replaced by a third Angel of the Lord.
- The only correct way to pray—and be heard!
- The secret Bible code which no one else has deciphered! What it means to your life and future events!
- The true meaning of crop circles and other unexplained phenomena!
- How you can "channel" the spirit of God and use other techniques of "spiritualism" for divine purposes.
- And much more.

What would you give for this divine knowledge? It has cost me a lifetime of labor. God always asks a token: a sacrifice of some sort—be it our labor, service, or (the symbol of our labor): a material gift—as a symbol of our dedication to God and the truth. I have been charged with the fearsome responsibility of not only disseminating this spiritual food (the very knowledge of the secrets of God) but also of gathering tokens in His praise.

So, it is up to you: are you a sheep or are you a goat? Do you want the complete knowledge of God's Divine Plan of the Ages (of which Pastor Russell had only the earliest glimpse) or do you want to live (and die) in darkness? The choice is all yours, but I guarantee that you won't be disappointed if you choose God.

As is customary in material exchanges, I have arranged for you to receive a material gift in exchange for your token. This surprise gift has brought countless blessings to many, and it is yours if you send me your token before midnight tomorrow.

How much should the token be? Well, that is between you and God. What is the knowledge of God worth to you? What is your everlasting life worth to you? Jesus said "Sell all that you have," but you need to decide what sort of a gift would be appropriate. Just be aware that if God decides that the token is too small, God will reject it as an insult. One joker recently sent $50—God instructed me to send it right back to him. Don't make the same mistake he did! Don't let your offering be an insult to your Creator!

Act today.

The decision is yours.

God's knowledge awaits

Choose wisely

Use PayPal.